IN THE MISTY BLUE YONDER

IN THE MISTY BLUE YONDER

And Other Mysteries from Southern Appalachia

TREY LETCHER

ISBN-13: 978-1-7367878-2-3 (*Paperback*)
ISBN-13: 978-1-7367878-3-0 (*E-Book*)

For Randy

TABLE OF
CONTENTS

A PLACE ON
THE WATER

D ONNA HEARD KEYS jingling outside the front door. She checked her watch. 10:40 p.m. It was safe to assume that by this hour, her husband was seeing at least two of everything. This would explain the exasperating amount of time it was taking him to get the key into the keyhole.

Eventually, Ray Solomon made entry into his home. From the kitchen, Donna watched him stagger through the foyer, heading straight for their bedroom at the back of the house. She went to the entrance, removed the keys he'd left dangling in the lock, and closed the door he'd left standing wide open. She returned to the kitchen, took his dinner plate from the microwave, and began scraping the cold contents into the garbage. After stacking his plate on top of hers and Julie's in the big farmhouse sink, she poured a small amount of Malbec into a glass and went onto the back patio. She sat quietly for half an hour sipping the wine, then, reluctantly, went back inside.

There was no sign of Ray in the bedroom. The bed was neat and empty and the en-suite unoccupied. She heard a noise in their walk-in closet, switched on the light, and opened the door. Ray lay sprawled on the floor in the back corner. Beneath him were her expensive dress heels and collection of knee-high leather and suede boots. He snored softly, still in his work clothes. She closed the closet door, turned off the light, brushed her teeth, changed into her Titans nightshirt, and climbed into their king-sized bed.

• • •

The next morning, Ray had left for work by 6:00 a.m. He'd showered in the guest bathroom and taken a handful of Excedrin with his coffee. Still unsteady from the previous night's old fashioneds, he opened the door to his fifteen-year-old's bedroom and stood there silently, feeling remorse swell within him. When she stirred, he turned quickly and eased the door closed.

Outside, he found his car parked halfway into one of his wife's cherished flower beds.

Driving north on I-65, excerpts from the previous night flashed in and out of his mind. He remembered leaving the Oak Bar and heading to the parking garage on Commerce Street. Then he was at the Renaissance Bridge Bar, where the television on the wall above the rows of bottles was tuned to a Predators away game. Then, he was on I-65 South. Bright lights in his rearview. Windows down. Screaming. Speeding. Swerving. Horns. Another feeling came to him. This time, though, it was something more like gut-wrenching fear.

Ray turned up the volume on the stereo and caught a news alert on talk radio. "The Mustang apparently rolled several times then struck the pier column of an overpass heading south on Interstate Sixty-Five in Williamson County," the announcer said stoically. "The driver was pronounced dead at the scene. Multiple eyewitnesses described the white Ford Mustang as racing with, or possibly being chased by, a black sport vehicle. Thus far, no one has come forward with a detailed description of the black vehicle which may have been involved."

Ray felt his stomach stir. His armpits were now damp. He switched the channel to a popular rush-hour morning show.

"Listen, we're talkin' a Shelby GT500," the DJ explained. "I mean, there can't be many cars around that'll keep up with that beast. If they were indeed going…you know…bumper to bumper, that narrows down the prospects. I mean, we can, with confidence, rule out, say…the mighty Prius?"

Laughter from the cohost, who then chimed in, "If you operate a Prius, please know you are in the clear."

The host continued, "Uh…let's see…how 'bout the Corvair."

More laughter from the cohost. "Remember the old Tennessee trash commercial?"

"Those operating a Corvair. Tennessee trash. Rest easy. You will not be questioned."

"Come on, now…let's…" the cohost interjected, stifling another laugh. "We gotta stop. Gotta stop. I mean, this poor guy got *decapitated*. Right? Let's show some respect. This is apparently a case of road rage taken to the—"

"All right, all right," the host acquiesced. "I mean, jeez. People. Loyal, beloved listeners, take it easy out there on the streets, will ya? I mean, from what we know, a-apparently, these two vehicles were really after one another. Zigzagging, horns blaring. Road raging. So just…people…keep a cool head out there, will ya?"

There was a second of silence before host and cohost burst into laughter.

Ray pulled onto the shoulder, pushed open the door of his Mythos Black Audi R8, and violently emptied his stomach on the littered asphalt.

• • •

When Ray Solomon was eleven years old, a neighborhood friend named Denton told him a story he would never forget. Denton had a fraternal twin brother named Donnie. They were playing outside one steamy day during their long summer break. Denton was shirtless and barefoot, wearing only a pair of cutoff jean shorts. The boy's mother had tired of them running in and out of the house for water while she was cleaning the kitchen. She finally ordered them to drink from the hose beside the front porch.

So, with Denton holding the open end near his face, Donnie cranked the spigot. A seemingly endless stream of bees poured out of the hose carried by warm water.

Little Denton Hyde received so many stings, dozens, that a doctor told him he had developed an allergy. Subsequently, even a single sting could be fatal. Denton was the smaller, sicklier twin and already suffered a slew of health issues. He was on a significant regimen of medication. While recounting the story to Ray, he had articulated the word as if he were an MD: anaphylaxis.

In a wicked sort of irony, Ray had lost more in the six sober months following the accident than in all his years of steady intake. But considering his decades of recklessness, he was thankful to have gotten out with his life. As for the unsubstantiated bee story, Ray now felt a foreboding correlation between his little friend's precarious relationship with the buzzing insect and his own with alcohol. Just one little...

• • •

Coming off the bridge leading into Olivia, Ray decided he'd bypass the little historic lake town and continue along the scenic two-lane highway to his new hometown of Moreland in rural Myer County.

Ray found the road by memory and turned at the long-deserted square brick building. His realtor said it had once been the post office for the town of Cedar Crest, which now existed only in historical archives. The left side of the long road sloped down to the river and was populated by jagged rock formations, stands of lifeless-looking pines, and wild brush. On the right was thickly forested woodland. There would be few neighbors for him to deal with. Of the few sad-looking dwellings, Ray deemed most uninhabitable. He'd been told that his closest neighbor, who shared the cul-de-sac on the wooded side, was a middle-aged single man who was quiet and kept to himself. The neighbor's residence, Ray's realtor had added, was tucked deep into the woods, visible only during the winter months.

The marketing catchphrase had been: "A Unique Find." According to the listing, the piece of property Ray recently purchased boasted an eclectic history. Originally a Camp Fire Girls compound into the late seventies, it had later housed a waterfront restaurant for a few struggling years and, most recently, a health clinic that had been raided and padlocked at the height of the region's opioid crisis.

It was situated on a peaceful one-and-a-half-acre wooded lot at the end of Telegraph Lane, a historically disreputable road. Sparsely populated, the claustrophobic stretch of crumbling asphalt paralleled the shoreline. The property boasted over three hundred feet of lake frontage and included a boat dock. There was a 1,900-square-foot primary structure, plus a small, detached cinder block building with an air-conditioning unit in one of its small windows and a tangle of electrical wires climbing an exterior wall. His realtor presumed it to have been an activity space for the Camp Fire Girls.

As Ray cruised leisurely toward his new residence, there came a low rumble behind him. In his rearview, Ray watched several motorcycles quickly gaining on him until he lost sight of them behind the couch jutting out of the bed of his truck. Apparently in more of a hurry than Ray, the four of them thundered past him in double file formation on the narrow road and eventually disappeared around a bend.

As he approached the cul-de-sac, there was no sign of the bikers, only the lingering dust they'd stirred up in his new neighbor's dirt driveway. Ray could hear the gurgling Harley-Davidson engines somewhere within the camouflaged compound. "Quiet my ass," he whispered to his realtor. *Bitch.*

He turned left and pulled the Ford Sport Trac pickup—a recent purchase of less than nine thousand dollars—into his driveway. The primary structure, which would be Ray's new residence, resembled a small, boxlike school building. Out front, rusted handrails led up concrete steps to a double-doored front entrance. The gravel driveway curved around to the rear of the building to what had been a parking area during its commercial stints. There was a smaller set of steps leading to a single, narrow back door. Much of the white exterior paint had peeled away and now littered the over-grown landscape. Several windows remained overlaid with plywood. Beyond the ample space of the old parking area was a path leading down to a boat dock that reached out over Lake Olivia. The privacy and the lake view had done it for Ray, whose only happy childhood memories were the occasional fishing trips with his dad upon this very lake. The bargain price hadn't hurt.

He took the back steps and entered through the rear door,

which opened into the kitchen. The commercial appliances from its restaurant days had been replaced with more modest residential models. He went past the kitchen and through an open entranceway into the spacious main room—the *parlor* room, as his realtor had called it with a straight face. A large, wood-burning fireplace anchored the wall dividing the main room and the kitchen. The two side walls were covered in graffitied whitewashed paneling. On the left were doors to two small rooms, which might have been dorm rooms during its Camp Fire days, and the health clinic's examination rooms. Between the rooms was the sole restroom, which had a second poorly constructed exterior door added on. On the right was one other identical small room and a large utility closet.

Standing in the middle of the huge, empty, ugly *parlor* room, Ray felt a tinge of self-pity ripple through him.

• • •

That night Ray slept on the small sofa he'd single-handedly maneuvered off his truck and dragged into the middle of the main room. It was among the few necessities—along with Mr. Coffee and a cheap end table—he figured he'd need during the first week or so, until he could properly furnish the place.

Awakened by the earsplitting growl of more motorcycles, he got to his feet and hurried over to the front window. The noise subsided as he watched several weaving taillights disappear into the woods across the cul-de-sac.

He looked at his watch: 1:57 a.m. *You're fuckin' kidding me.*

• • •

Ray stepped from his back door into the misty dawn with a thermos full of fresh-brewed coffee. Examining his new property, he noted that, indeed, the slope was "gentle" from the parking area down to the lake, and there was plenty of "wooded privacy" providing the lucky owner—him—the sense of "peaceful sanctuary."

A not-so-gentle slope led up to the edge of the woods, where the small white cinder block building sat in stark contrast against a deep-green forest backdrop. Ray climbed the narrow trail to the structure and tried to open its door, but something prohibited his entry. He pushed harder, and the door began to give with an unpleasant scraping sound. With the door partway open, he could see the end of a metal frame of bunk beds. His heart jumped when he noticed the dirty bottoms of two slender feet at the end of the lower bunk. Ray stuck his head inside far enough to make out a female form sleeping soundly. She wore a dingy flannel shirt and dark sweatpants, her arms folded to cushion her head. A shock of dark disheveled hair veiled her face, but he could make out a mouth slightly agape.

"Hello," Ray said softly. Getting no response, he repeated, "Hello. Miss?"

A startled eye sprung open, then the woman rolled off the bed onto the floor and quickly scooted backwards on her bottom until she met the far wall. Her hair still covered most of her face.

"It's okay. You're okay," Ray said, trying to dispel her obvious fear. "I just bought this place. So...it's been vacant a while. Have you been staying here?"

"No. I don't stay here...I...I'm leaving. Will you just...let me go? Please?"

"Of course. Are you okay?"

"I'm fine." She got to her feet, keeping her head low, and cautiously moved to the middle of the room. She stood there a moment in clothes that were obviously much too large, nervously opening and closing her hands. "You gonna let me through?"

"Yes. Yes."

She began pulling the bed frame away from the door. Ray stepped back, allowing her to pass. Then, he stood there, disconcerted, watching her walk unhurriedly into the woods toward the biker's property.

When she was gone, he walked down toward the water and stepped onto the boat dock. He turned around and stared up at the little block building, uneasy, not sure what he expected to see. After a moment, he took a sip of coffee and began to examine the dock.

It was in worse shape than he remembered during his initial inspection. The loose nails he'd replace with screws. The dry-rotted rubber bumpers along its edges were missing entire sections. But that should be easy enough to mend, he reckoned. He slid his hands in his pockets and watched the occasional boat pass by. Most were small fishing vessels. Locals, he figured, returning from early morning angling before the temperature hit its noontime projection of ninety-two degrees.

•••

Ray spent Saturday doing chores around the place. Before he could tame the yard, he needed to haul away the piles of junk and debris. He grudgingly toiled outside in the late-June humidity, making three trips to the county dump.

By early evening, he was exploring inside with the wall-mounted heat-and-air unit set for maximum cooling. In the utility closet, aside from leftover cleaning equipment, a water heater, and empty wire shelves, he discovered the attic access. He pulled the chain to lower the door and unfolded the hinged wooden ladder, then climbed into the dark, stifling space that smelled like raw earth. He found a single light bulb mounted just above his head as he stepped onto the plywood floor. The big, open room was sparse, save for a stack of boxes in one corner. To his left, along what was the front of the house, he noticed custom-built cubby holes along the entire wall, possibly a hundred or more of assorted sizes, painted black. Using his cell phone for added illumination, Ray searched the cubbies, finding loose nuts and bolts, boxes of nails, light bulbs, rolls of black electrical tape, paint cans, and various other maintenance items. From one space, he removed a white plastic garbage bag sealed with a rubber band that broke when he pulled at it. Inside, Ray discovered thirty or so faded Polaroid pictures of topless and otherwise naked women. Each photo showed a different female posing seductively for the camera. The one constant being they were all sitting or reclining upon a medical examination table against a whitewashed paneled wall. Shaking his head, Ray studied each photo a second time, then placed them back inside the bag and pushed it deep into the cubby.

He knelt by the boxes on the floor and began rifling through them. These contained relics from Camp Fire Girls, mostly manuals, maps of regional hiking trails, and reams of miscellaneous paperwork. He took out a booklet titled *Book of Camp Fire Girls*, its simplistic cover showing a rendering of two Camp Fire Girls walking with their arms around one another, each outfitted in her blue skirt and hat, crisp white shirt, and red kerchief. Along the right edge was a column of graphics, the organization's icons or badge emblems, Ray guessed. As sweat began rolling into his eyes, he dropped the booklet and wiped his face and neck with his shirt tail. He straightened with a groan and made his way back to the access.

Ray pulled the chain on the light and descended the ladder. In the kitchen, he downed a small bottle of water, then collapsed on the couch and remained there until morning sunlight flooded the room.

• • •

The next afternoon, Sunday, Ray left the cul-de-sac intending to drive to the town of Olivia, but then he remembered the little marina with an on-site restaurant his realtor—if he still believed a word from her mouth—had promised served great down-home cooking.

He took the two-lane highway and, before long, saw the sign for Whispering Winds Marina. The road leading to the marina was narrow, and Ray had to veer onto the shoulder to make room for an oncoming truck trailering a bowrider. It then took a ninety-degree turn to the left and elevated slightly with the marina entrance on the right at the crest. Ray turned in and saw the restaurant directly ahead. Parking was to the right, near a massive steel building used for dry boat storage. The marina itself was a ways beyond that. The quaint sky-blue building with white trim might have been a tiny Victorian cottage were it not for the sign over the door: OFFICE.

The diner's exterior sufficiently embodied its moniker, the Rusty Anchor, with unpretentious authenticity. Its cedar siding had weathered gray, the deck a patchwork of bowed, splintered original planks with a scattering of newer replacements. Ray opened the screen door and peeked inside, triggering a clanking cowbell above his head.

"Hello," a raspy female voice called.

Ray looked around for the source of the greeting. Just inside on the left was a long counter with an unmanned cash register. Behind sliding glass panels were shelves filled with stacks of baseball caps and neatly folded T-shirts, both available for $16.99. There was but a single color to choose from, light-blue, and the sample on display boasted the Rusty Anchor logo—which might have been created by a young child or an artistically challenged adult—imprinted in an ill-conceived blood-red ink.

"You can sit inside or out," the same voice offered.

Ray scanned the small dining room, which seemed cramped. There was movement in his periphery; someone had passed behind the long, rectangular opening looking into the kitchen. Then through a swinging door came an attractive young woman, perhaps a few years older than his daughter. She wore a straw cowboy hat and the tank-top version of the diner's signature sky-blue shirt, which, Ray noticed, contrasted nicely against the long, dark-brown hair falling in waves over her shoulders.

"Hi. O-okay," Ray stammered. "I'll try the deck."

"Okay, sir, we'll get a menu out to ya," the young woman said with a pretty smile and dimpled cheeks. Her eyes were bright and green, with a subtle scattering of freckles beneath them. Ray found himself appreciating her attractiveness in the passive way he had the youthful vibrancy of his own daughter's friends who frequented the home he once inhabited.

Outside, Ray took a stool along the heavily varnished

wood counter that ran the perimeter of the deck. Waiting for his menu, he watched a family—mom, dad, and young daughter—preparing their little Bayliner for an outing. Mom secured the girl's life vest, positioned her on the bench seat beside the cockpit, then went forward herself and took a seat in the bow. Father released the lines, took his position at the helm, and slowly reversed out of the covered slip. He idled past the restaurant, giving Ray a wave, which Ray returned. A second greeting went to the marina employee standing on the dock by the fuel pumps. After clearing the "No Wake Zone," the captain accelerated his vessel through the cove, turned into the channel, and disappeared.

Ray heard the screen door slam and watched a scruffy teenaged-looking kid coming toward him with a laminated menu and silverware wrapped in a paper napkin.

He consumed a pulled pork sandwich, a side of potato salad, and multiple glasses of delicious fresh-squeezed lemonade.

After paying the waiter, Ray stood and stretched, then turned to leave just as a gentleman stepped onto the deck holding a piece of paper in his hand. He walked over to a shadow box attached to the restaurant's exterior wall, opened the glass, and thumbtacked the paper to the back of the box. He closed the glass just as Ray came beside him.

"Nice boat," Ray said, looking over the man's shoulder.

"Priced at a bargain. Motivated seller if you're in the hunt," the man said, grinning. He had a leathery tanned face with deep creases along his mouth and forehead. He could have been a young sixty-year-old or a fortysomething who'd spent too much time in the harsh Dixie sun.

"Yeah? Let's see." Ray scanned the flyer. "Out of my ballpark," he said, eyeing the $38,000 price. He extended his hand. "Ray Solomon."

"Bo Shula, co-owner. Harbormaster," the man said, nodding toward the marina office building. Then, aiming a thumb at the restaurant, "Part-time bus boy and full-time cleaner of the men's room." He grinned again, his face filling with lines. "Are you lookin'?"

"Thinkin' about it," Ray said. "Just moved into the place at the end of Telegraph Lane. My dock's seen better days, but it's hangin' on."

"Oh, okay. I know the place. Nice piece of property. I was glad to see it finally rezoned residential. That road has a reputation. Used to be a sleazy little strip club about midways down. Finally bulldozed that a few years ago. The dilapidated apartment building behind where it was, the guy with the club owned that too. Lotta the dancers stayed there. He kept 'em doped up, dependent on those tips." Bo shook his head. "Hope they level it too."

Ray nodded. "I noticed. Not easy on the eyes."

"And I'm sure you know about your property's latest enterprise?"

"Mm-hmm." Ray snickered. "I was clued in later. They left it off the webpage."

"Imagine," Bo said with a tilted head and crooked grin. "The doctor, Rosselli, still practices in Olivia. State surgeon general barred him from writing scripts for certain...I guess...controlled substances. For a short time. But they never really *nailed* him." Bo waved a hand and shook his head. "Anyway," he checked his watch, "I'm officially off for the day. My half day Sunday. Can I buy you a welcome-to-the-neighborhood beer?"

Ray held up his hands. "No, thanks. Abstaining. But I'll be back for more of that lemonade."

Just then, the pretty girl walked toward them carrying a Corona bottle topped with a lime wedge. Bo took it from her. "Thank you, sweetie." He ran the cold bottle along his hairline. "Cookout. Tomorrow. Seven," he said, then flipped the bill of her hat with a finger. "Be there, cowgirl."

She smiled and began pulling triggers on her imaginary six-shooters.

"You met Ray?" Bo asked.

"I did, but...didn't get your name. Sorry."

"She's not nearly as hospitable as me," Bo said. "Or as good lookin.'"

"Right. I'm a mean, ugly one." She offered her hand. "Elise." Her smile brought out the dimples again.

"Ray bought the property at the end of Telegraph Lane," Bo said.

"Oh, wow."

Ray wondered what Elise's "wow" might imply. He studied her face, the long dark hair spilling out of the cowboy hat. He registered her height and general build. Recognition sank in.

She asked, "You from around here?"

"Nashville area. But I spent my early years on this river. Down a ways."

"Oh yeah?" Bo said.

According to Ray's mother, his father was useless as a husband, a "rounder" she'd called him. But even by her account, Stan Solomon adored his son.

"Yeah, my dad took me on overnight trips up and down the Tsugama. I remember we'd anchor in a cove around dusk and eat peanut butter sandwiches and Pringles on the little round plastic table. Afterwards, we'd cast out, secure the rods...there were two rod holders on the side...and just wait around for the big one to bite."

Ray would drink canned RC Colas from the cooler while Stan poured cheap blended whiskey into a clear plastic cup. They both peed into the water when the need arose, as the head below deck was perpetually nonfunctioning. His father wouldn't say much. The more he drank, in fact, the quieter he became. But he would smile at his son, showing Red Man–stained teeth, the scar from a bar fight spreading wide and white below his lip. When little Ray got tired, he'd disappear into the dark cabin, lie in front of the battery-powered fan, and watch the stars through the bow window tilted open above his head.

"Sea Ray," he blurted out as the logo entered his mind's eye. Ray tried to recall the silly thing his father had said concerning their shared name. Failing to do so, he continued, "Yeah, with the, ah...the room below."

"Yeah?" Bo said, his brow arched.

"Yeah. I'd like something like that. I'd enjoy the nostalgia. Cheap, of course. But dependable. I'm not much when it comes to engines."

"I'll let you boys talk boats," Elise said, flashing Ray an expression of gratitude. "So, I expect to see you around, Mr. Ray."

"Absolutely."

He watched as she sauntered away. *Same walk.*

"This whole thing is a family venture," Bo said. "My parents had it, now me and my wife, the chef. Elise is my niece. We're kinda helping her out. She's been through some stuff. Sweet kid, big heart. But she's a rascal."

"I've got one similar," Ray admitted.

Bo nodded sympathetically, then gave the lime a squeeze and pushed it into the bottle with his finger. He took a long drink, licked his lips, and continued. "Her mom, my older sister, is in Virginia. She wasn't much interested in the marina biz, so she sold out to me.

"Oh..." Bo pointed at Ray. "I know a guy, Connor, more of a yacht broker, but he can find anything. Should be able to come up with something close to what you want. An older model Sea Ray cuddy cabin. Don't see many of those around. Got no air-conditioning. Too damned hot here. But he's got connections all over the place. He can have it transported for a fee."

"Great. Thanks," Ray said.

"I'll give him a ring..." Bo promised, "get him on it."

"Okay," Ray said. "Well, you'll be seeing a lot of me. Great food..." He gestured toward the mountains beyond the cove. "Great view. And that lemonade."

•••

On Monday, Ray drove to the Rusty Anchor only to find it to be the one day of the week both it and the marina were closed.

Back at his new home, he walked down to the boat dock, removed his phone from the pocket of his shorts, and Face-Timed his daughter. To his surprise, she answered.

"Hi, Julie, just wanted to see your ugly face."

"Hi, Dad," she replied with a yawn. She'd obviously not yet removed herself from her comfy bed to begin the day's activities, whatever they may be. Her messy hair covered most of her face.

"Except...I still can't see you," Ray said, bringing his phone closer.

She took a hand and ran it front to back through her long blonde hair.

"There you are."

"Here I am," she said, rolling her eyes.

"Survived my first weekend here. Wanna see the view?"

She yawned again and replied wryly, "Oookay."

Ray turned the phone toward the water and scanned the lake. "That's right off my dock." He turned around and provided her a view of the property.

"Okay, yuck," she said flatly.

"It's more about the location." *And price.* "Lakefront. But yeah, it definitely needs some...like...*Rehab Addict*."

"Speaking of...Mom said you just stopped going."

Ray hesitated, then said, "I didn't call to talk about... I wanted to see you and see what you were up to."

"So, you didn't bail?"

"Sweetie, I went. I did it. And I'm glad I did it. Scared the hell out of me."

Julie began looking around, as if suddenly bored with the conversation.

"How's your mom?"

"The spy? She's fine."

"What's that mean?"

"It means she constantly spies on me. Goes through my phone. My laptop..."

"Oh. Well, does—"

"Dad, Stacy's trying to call me. We're making plans for my birthday trip."

"Okay, sweetie."

"My name is Julie."

"Okay, *Julie*. Hey, call me later. Tonight. Tell me what you and Stacy cook up. If you need any ideas, there's picturesque Lake Olivia over here on the eastern end of the state."

Julie rolled her eyes again, but a hint of a smile tugged at the corner of her mouth. "Bye, Dad."

"Bye. Love you. Hey, I'm getting a boat—"

Julie's face disappeared from the screen.

• • •

"Good news," Bo hollered, walking up to Ray in the marina parking lot, the sheet of paper he held flapping in the breeze. "We got a hit. It's a small cuddy cabin. Good shape. A few marks on the hull, some flaws in the decals. What you'd expect from an older boat. Other than that, she's nice."

"That was quick," Ray said, caught off guard. "What else do you know about it?"

"I printed this for you." Bo handed Ray the flyer. "Got the cabin you wanted. Sink and head below. Rod holders aft."

Ray skimmed the boat's bulleted features:

- 2000 Sea Ray 215 Express Cruiser
- Good condition
- Single owner, kept in dry storage
- 21.5 ft.
- 2015 MerCruiser 5.0L engine (very low hours on engine)
- Bimini top and cover
- Trailer included
- $12,000

"Owner says he'll drive it over here from Olivia anytime. Let us do a sea trial. Guy recently moved down from the Great Lakes area. In fact, he was on one of those reality shows, like you see on the Discovery Channel. Something about 'big catch' or something. Connor says the price is good, especially with the newer engine, and the guy kept all the paperwork too. Every little thing. Of course, Connor does a thorough inspection before he agrees to list anything. It's kept up at the Smoky Cove Marina. Like I said before, too hot down here, guy wants something with an open bow. Felt like the cabin was wasted space. You're *sure* you want the enclosed bow?"

"Yeah. Let's have a look at it."

"Okay. Any particular time good for you?"

"Anytime," Ray said.

Bo pulled a phone from his pocket. "What's your number?"

• • •

Later that evening Ray got a call from Bo; he answered on his way to the back porch.

"He can run it down here tomorrow, early. That work?" Bo asked.

"Sure. How does your wife do with breakfast?"

"Best around. I suggest the country ham platter. You won't eat the rest of the day."

Ray's phone beeped and he checked the screen. "Hey, Bo, I need to take another call. I appreciate this. I'll be there bright and early."

"All right. See you tomorrow."

Ray switched over. "Hey there."

"Hey," Donna said.

A pause.

"I...talked to Julie," Ray said. "Is it me, or is she becoming more delightful by the day?"

Donna scoffed. "Isn't she? She couldn't wait to tell me that your new place is a dump."

"You sit her down and explain that divorce and unemployment have consequences. Make it a teachable moment."

"Maybe I shouldn't mention what kind of car Julie has decided on for her sweet sixteen."

"Correct. Not the best time."

"Look..." Donna hesitated. "Daddy has already said he wants to buy her—"

"Daddy *is* going to buy her a car. *Her* daddy!"

"Whoa. You weren't kidding. Another time." She took a deep breath. "How is everything else?"

"Sobriety sucks. I'm packin' on weight. I actually think society is more accepting of drunks than fat people."

"I've lived with you drunk. I'd rather you'd've been fat."

"Good. Because I have a new addiction. Lemonade, fresh-squeezed by caring hands at the Rusty Anchor restaurant."

"Lemonade at the Rusty Anchor? Is that a lateral move from a house old fashioned at the Oak Bar?"

"A step up, actually."

"Yeah. Sounds like it," Donna said. "Well, good. Drink your sugary lemonade and be fat and happy. Your next wife will find you much easier to tolerate."

"That's what I'll do, Counselor. If I learned anything in rehab, it's that 'there are only two kinds of drunks, happy and angry.' I was not a giddy sot."

"Oh stop, Ray."

"And that I had been engaged for quite a number of years in what those in the field refer to as *maintenance* drinking."

"Ray."

"And…when I drank heavily, which, you may remember, I did on occasion, it often elicited inner indignation, irritability, rage, and other fun and exciting things. After all, alcohol brought about disinhibition, and trouble…uh…what was it? Trouble suppressing my urges. Which were, quite possibly, murderous."

"Please don't, Ray."

"By the way. Are we still on the same script? You wouldn't roll over on your daughter's father, would you?" Ray asked.

"No. I can't envision Julie visiting you in prison. She may not visit you, period."

"Well, let's give thanks for partial blackouts…another symptom. I can't truthfully say that I ran someone into a concrete bridge, not with any certainty. Thank God I was drunk."

"Let's drop it," she said in a broken whisper. She paused a moment. "I *called* to tell you we have an offer on the house. We have a buyer. Better now, butthole?"

"Language."

After another pause, Donna said confidently, "We'll both be fine after we close."

"You'll be fine no matter, daddy's girl." With immediate regret, Ray took a deep breath and exhaled slowly. "I've got one last face-to-face with that firm on Thursday. If they bring me on, it won't be until the end of August. Salary's about half. Although, as Julie can attest, I've downgraded my lifestyle significantly. But enough depressing talk. It's too pretty a night. I'm watching the sunset."

"Julie *did* admit you had a decent view of the lake."

"Yeah, if I just keep my head turned that way… I'm actually seeing a guy about a boat tomorrow."

"A boat *and* a place on the water? Did you have something socked away you failed to disclose to my lawyer?"

"*Your* lawyer? Even if I'd crammed it up my ass..."

She scoffed. "What do you know about boats?"

"If you can drive a car... And, FYI, she's old and very cheap."

"Daddy says they're expensive to maintain."

"Yes, I'm sure your father's sixty-foot yacht requires a fair bit of scratch to keep shipshape."

"Well, stock it with plenty of sunscreen," Donna said dryly.

Ray snorted and examined his pale, freckled forearms.

• • •

Wednesday morning, Ray had a hearty breakfast out on the Rusty Anchor's deck. This time, Elise waited on him. The subject of their bizarre, initial encounter at his little cinder block building was not broached.

Ray paid the bill and sat for a moment drinking coffee until he noticed the Express Cruiser idling through the cove toward the marina. He watched its operator, who Ray assumed was the owner, expertly navigate the boat into a tight spot along the dock between two other vessels. As he tied the lines, he was met by Bo and another gentleman. Connor the broker, Ray reckoned.

He secured a five-dollar bill under his empty coffee cup and made his way toward the dock, knowing he was buying the boat without ever needing to board her.

The bill of sale was executed online in the marina's office. The owner, a Mr. Ryan Sandstone, graciously agreed to pull the trailer down that weekend and drop it off at the marina. Sandstone caught a ride back to Olivia in Connor the broker's FJ Cruiser.

"You can keep it here," Bo said of the trailer. "The field behind the dry storage building. It's fenced and locked. It'll be fine there. Just make sure you come and push it around every now and then, keep the tires rotated."

"Thanks, Bo." Ray handed over the keys to his truck.

"Sure," Bo said taking the keys. "Okay, the missus and I will be there waiting. She'll have to bring me right back; one of my guys called in sick. But soon, you'll have to take me out on her."

Ray's face portrayed guarded excitement. "Guess my first trip will be solo."

"Just take it nice and easy until you get her insured."

"Well, this outing should take all of, what, four minutes?"

Bo laughed. "Already stackin' the hours on that replacement engine." Then he pointed a finger at Ray. "Oh, I meant to tell you, there's a submerged house not far off your dock. Its chimney can be a real hazard, depending on your draft and the water level."

"My draft?"

"The depth of your hull below the waterline. We're at the mercy of the mighty dam here. Water's up until around the first of November when they begin lowering it in increments. The stone chimney shows itself pretty well then. Right now, it'd be hard to spot. Just come at your dock wide and approach on the far side, your starboard side. Safe travels, Skipper."

Ray wrestled the big floating keychain from his pocket and headed for the boat. He backed aboard using the narrow gunwale steps to avoid taking the long, awkward leap from the dock to the boat's carpeted deck. He opened the little sliding door to the cabin and went below. Its layout was identical to his father's, the smell just as he remembered. He returned topside, slid the door closed, and secured the latch. At the helm, he started the engine and looked around making sure he wasn't missing anything. He noticed the clip to the kill engine switch hanging from a red curly cord beside him. He grabbed it and tethered it to the waistband of his shorts as Bo recommended, "Especially when you're out alone."

Luckily, the boat that had been in front of his had departed, giving Ray much-needed room to maneuver away from the dock. As he throttled forward then back to neutral, he noticed a whining sound not present during the sea trial. Gliding slowly through the "No Wake Zone," he tried the stereo using the controls at the helm but couldn't get it working. He was sure Connor had tested it for him; he even recalled a Chris Stapleton song coming from the Clarion speakers.

Apart from these issues, the boat handled easily, and he was able to get it on plane for a brief time before his dock came into view.

Bo was walking down the slope of Ray's property as Ray made his initial approach. Recognizing the unfortunate angle Ray had taken, Bo hurried onto the dock to help. Ray shifted from neutral to reverse, working the steering wheel. The more effort he made to align the boat with the dock, the more skewed she got. He finally circled around and came at it again, thrusting between forward and neutral. The whining sound persisted.

"Keep it in neutral and let the current bring you in," Bo called to him. "Keep it slow. Slow and steady."

"All right," Ray yelled, but continued to overwork the wheel.

"Steering's all but useless when you're coasting. The wind's up today. It'll get you here."

Ray obediently stopped fighting and simply stood behind the wheel as she floated up to the dock. Bo put a foot on the bow rail to stop the momentum, then manhandled her to get her straight.

"Go ahead and cut the engine and the blower."

Ray did so.

"Toss those fenders over."

Ray palmed each of the black fenders that lay inside the rail and dropped them over the gunwale.

"Now, toss me your lines. Stern first."

Ray went aft and threw the line Bo's way. As Bo secured it to the cleat, Ray made his way forward and grabbed the neatly coiled bowline. He tried tying the line himself, looping it repeatedly around the cleat.

"You gotta show me the right way to tie onto these things," Ray said, embarrassed.

"No problem," Bo said. "You know the saying, 'If you can't tie a knot, tie a lot.'"

Ray laughed. He was beginning to appreciate the veteran boatman's patience and easygoing manner.

"You might wanna keep some lines tied on the dock as well," Bo suggested. "Be quicker and easier."

"Okay," Ray said. "Some of the accessories aren't working. Couldn't get the stereo to play. The gauges. And something's grinding when I shift into neutral."

Bo finished securing the stern line and straightened. "Permission to come aboard?"

Ray grinned. "Please."

Bo stepped onto the deck and scanned the helm. He pulled the key from the ignition. "You're using the wrong key," Bo said, holding up a key by its long, black grip. "This is for the gas tank cap. Surprised it even started her."

"Let me see," Ray said, leaning in.

"This small one, with the Sea Ray logo, that's your ignition key." Bo took the small key, inserted it, and turned the engine over. He punched the stereo controls, and soon Chris Stapleton's unmistakable voice filled the cockpit. "Guess the CD was part of the package."

Ray offered Bo a self-conscious smile.

"How'd it go?" a lady called down. She was standing beside Bo's blue SUV, shielding her face from the sun with a hand.

"Ray, my wife Jeanne," Bo said, then yelled up at her, "Jeanne, Ray."

"Good to meet you," Ray hollered. Then, with all the amiability he could muster, "And let's just say you're a damned better cook than I am a boatman."

"Nah, he's gonna be great," Bo countered reassuringly.

• • •

It was early evening when Donna called. Ray pulled the phone from his pocket and made his way to the front porch as he answered.

"Hey."

"Hello," Donna said. "Not great news. Are you up for it?"

"Hit me."

"Your daughter is in quite the relationship. I'll spare you details from the texts I've discovered between her and this kid."

"Okay."

"Thing is, he's a good kid. It's Julie who's...apparently...pushing him to..."

Ray took a deep breath and exhaled.

"I also found a couple of loose pills in the pocket of her shorts. Blue. God knows what they were. Oh, and apparently, I'm no longer Julie's *mom*. I'm the *bitch*. As in, 'The *bitch* won't be back until three o'clock. Hurry over...'"

"I bought a boat."

Donna couldn't stifle her laugh. "Well...that's good. And highly relevant to this conversation."

"So, you *are* spying on her?"

"I am monitoring our daughter's text conversations. I'm doing the best I can on my own."

"Who is this *fucking* kid?" Ray blurted, the seriousness of the issue hitting him.

"Forget it. I'll buy her some condoms to keep in her purse. Do they still show that educational film in school? With the banana—"

"Enough."

"Well..." She paused. "This has been constructive. Oh, before I wish you good night and sweet dreams... The buyers, they vamoosed. Found something that *suited* them better."

"That's golden," Ray said. "You should've started with that."

"Well, I was sitting on such a cache of good news," Donna said, "I didn't know where to begin."

"Thanks for calling."

"No, please..." Donna mused. "Thank you for your solace."

Ray moved the phone away from his ear and tapped the red button.

He walked back into the main room and stood looking around. He was noticing in himself an uneasiness when inside his new home. It was cold and stark. And depressing. It suddenly struck him that he'd been bumbling around with no real purpose. Lacking a single meaningful aspiration. Impotent. He thought about taking a trip to the attic for stimulus in a white plastic bag. But then, his eyes wandered over the end table, where lay his wallet and the boat keys, and his thoughts wavered. Finally, figuring he had a couple of hours of daylight left, he gathered his things and walked out the back door without closing it behind him.

Bo had told him the Smoky Cove Tavern and Marina was a straight shot up the main channel, with the only real turn being that which led into the cove. "Look for the big white house on the tip of the peninsula. Which, coincidentally, is the residence of our good friend Dr. Andrew Rosselli. Take a right into the cove. It's a nice little trip."

• • •

The big white house stood bright and stately, flanked by stands of tall pines. Ray veered into the cove, rounded the peninsula, and eased back on the throttle. Several other grand estates dotted the shore of Olivia's Old Town on his right. Along the left shore, dwellings of humbler pedigree, mostly darkly stained A-frames, and small cedar cottages, sat far back in their heavily wooded properties.

He idled along the Riverwalk lined with an attractive nautical rope barrier. The marina came up on his right with its rustic-looking restaurant—three times the size of the Rusty Anchor—overlooking the marina from the high bank.

He was able to tie up at the near end of the dock. There were no cleats, so he wrapped his lines around a piling and secured them with overhand knots. He walked down the dock and up the long wooden stairway to the restaurant's back patio, then entered its barroom.

He knew he was going to drink without ever having given it a conscious thought.

•••

Ray awakened at the sound of motorcycle engines. When he sat up on the couch, the room spun. He closed his eyes and let the waves of movement subside. When he stood and began shuffling toward the front door, there was the sound of clinking glass. Something connected with his foot and slid across the floor.

Another motorcycle approached. He hurried to get the door open so he could confront the bikers about the noise. He stumbled onto the porch as the bike slowly approached the cul-de-sac. The driver of the Harley carried a passenger on the seat behind him, whose long dark hair hung down from a head that rolled and bounced as if attached by a spring. Her arms were wrapped around the driver, wrists tied together with something red. As they came even with Ray, he could see that the woman's legs were also wrapped around the driver, her pale bare feet resting atop the gas tank. He squinted, then opened his eyes wide, trying to focus as the driver leaned away and turned onto his neighbor's dirt driveway.

Ray yelled out, "Hey!" He could barely hear his own voice over the sound of the bike's grumble. As the taillight disappeared into wooded seclusion, Ray looked down and realized he was naked.

He ran inside and found his shorts on the floor near the couch surrounded by several tiny glass liquor bottles. He pulled them on and took off through the front door, crossed the cul-de-sac, and down his neighbor's driveway, weaving wildly. As he came upon the little house, he slowed to a stagger, stopped, and let the waves of nausea roll over him. He felt he might vomit but was able to stave it off.

The home was thirty yards into the thick forest. There were no exterior lights, just a hint of moonlight. Still, Ray could make out three big bikes leaned side by side near the front door. The old stone cottage was small and well kept. And except for the wrought iron bars over the windows and front door, it seemed wholesome, as if a sweet old grand-mother might reside there.

The front door was ajar; Ray stumbled inside. Sweat rolled from his hairline, stinging his eyes. He hollered between erratic breaths, "Let the... Let the girl go!"

A short, portly man emerged from a room on Ray's left. The man held up his hands submissively. "Take it easy, brother."

Ray ran a hand over his face, clearing the perspiration. "What the f-*fuck* is going on with you all?"

Moaning came from the narrow hallway directly ahead of Ray. The men exchanged glances, and the stocky man lowered one of his raised hands toward his waist. Ray took off down the hallway. He noticed light from under a door. He twisted the knob and pushed it open, causing it to slam against the wall. Elise was sitting up against the headboard of a single bed. She was rubbing her wrists with her freed hands and moaning as her green eyes rolled under heavy lids. A man sat on the edge of the bed fiddling with the red bandana around her ankles. Another, who'd been sitting in a chair in the cor-ner of the room, sprang up, dropping the lit cigarette from his mouth, and rushed to block Ray from entering.

"I'm sorry, Les. I'm soooo sorrrryyyy," Elise slurred in her raspy voice.

Ray heard footsteps coming up behind him. He tried to

force his way in, but the man fronting him shoved him backwards into the other man, who quickly threw his left arm around Ray's neck and stuck the cold, smooth face of a knife blade against his cheek.

"No. No!" Elise pleaded. "No. No, Les. Don't let them hurt him." Her eyes, now wide and terrified, met Ray's. "Ray?"

The man named Les took the freed bandana, leaned to one side, and stuck it in the back pocket of his faded jeans. He stood and walked toward Ray, his bulky boots thudding on the hardwood floor. The other man in the room backed away, allowing Les to get in Ray's face.

"Lower it," Les said to the man with the knife.

The blade disappeared from Ray's field of vision, leaving him staring up at the shadowed face of the mysterious Les.

Les sniffed and declared, "You're canned." His face was dark and indistinct, silhouetted by the light from the bedroom.

"Ray," Elise called out. "I'm okay. I'm okay, Ray. J-just go home. Pleeease, Ray."

"Ray, huh?" Les said flatly. "Do what she says. Go home. You two can talk tomorrow. Now get on."

"I'm okay, Ray. Please go home," Elise begged.

Reluctantly, Ray turned and began meandering through the hallway followed closely by the man with the knife. Ray lost his balance and stumbled forward, then, overcompensating, he lurched backwards, colliding into the man behind him. The man shoved Ray hard, sending him tripping over his own feet and landing face-first on the hardwoods. Slowly, Ray got back on his feet. He was slumped over, touching the knee that had skidded along the floor and was now bleeding. Without straightening, Ray charged forward and was met with a quick, straight jab which landed directly on the bridge of his nose and returned him to the floor.

"Aw, shit," the man said, watching the dark fluid stream down Ray's chin. "Listen. Hey...listen, brother. You got the wrong idea. Okay? Ain't no one hurtin' no one 'round here. Got it?"

Ray's eyes welled up. He blew a mist of blood out his nostrils, then wiped his nose with the back of his hand.

"Go home, brother," the man whispered. "Sleep it off. Then come on back."

• • •

Ray jerked awake and squinted into the early morning sun pouring through the front windows. His entire head ached. As he looked around the room, things did not move at the correct speed. He couldn't focus. He laid his head back on the armrest. The dream he was having just before he woke returned to him in flashes: driving his boat on the lake. Boat rolling at the mercy of huge, ocean-sized swells. His dock straight ahead. Thrusting the throttle forward. Racing toward the dock. The boat rising and falling, the dock disappears, then is visible, then is gone, then it's there again. Each time, closer. At the crest of a huge swell. Plunging as if from the peak of some colossal wooden roller coaster.

Before allowing himself to crash into the dock, he'd awakened.

Ray decided he was not ready to be up and about. He closed his eyes again: Elise, in her straw cowboy hat. Red bandana covering the bottom half of her face, outlaw style. Chasing him around the deck of the Rusty Anchor, rapid-firing two shiny revolvers. In the outside men's room behind the restaurant. Opening the door to the stall to hide. Elise in the stall, her green eyes smiling above the red bandana. Raising both barrels toward his face.

Ray awakened with a jolt.

Again, he closed his eyes: A medical examination room. A naked woman sitting on the exam table. Platinum-blonde hair, dark roots. Pale skin. Large, round breasts. Red Camp Fire Girls kerchief around her neck. Her laughing at him. Her pouring blue pills into his open mouth. Sharp pain, cheeks overextending, nerves stretching, snapping. Pills dissolving into a thick blue milkshake. Swallowing hard. Holding her kerchief. Tying her feet together. Tying her hands. Crossing the ends around her neck. Pulling taut as the face of his ex-wife stares back at him.

Ray awakened long enough to roll over and fall asleep one last time: Light in the windows of his little cinder block building. Scaling the steep hill using all fours. Dry dirt crumbling in his hands, beneath his bare feet. Using holes in the bank to climb. Snake heads emerging from holes. Topping the hill. Flickering light in the windows. Orange-and-yellow curtains rippling in the breeze. Pushing hard to open the door. Huge blazing fire in the middle of the room. Girls in their red, white, and blue outfits. On their knees around the fire, leaning forward. Warming hands near the fire. Smiling with delight. Hands disappearing inside dancing flames. Julie looking away from the fire. Seeing him in the doorway. Rolling her eyes. Other girls laughing riotously at him. Julie turning to him. Lifting her arms. Both hands aflame.

Ray shot off the couch. Again, he found himself completely naked, dried blood smeared on his chest and stomach, his joints stiff and aching.

Taking inventory of his surroundings, he saw the nude

photos he'd discovered in the attic strewn about the floor among a slew of miniature liquor bottles.

He pulled on his shorts, sans underwear, walked into the utility closet, and found the attic access ladder fully extended with drops of blood on its rungs.

His ringtone sounded. He found his phone between the couch cushions. Donna. It was 10:24 a.m.

"I'm guessing you had quite a night," she began.

"Mean—" He cleared phlegm from his throat. "Meaning?"

"Yuck."

"Sorry."

"Have you had a chance to check your text messages?"

A wave of dread came over him. He ended the call without replying.

From midnight until nearly one in the morning, there was a flurry of text messages to and from his ex-wife, as well as several to their daughter. As he swiped through, Ray felt a surge of apprehension. At some point, he'd begun sending texts to Julie that were meant for Donna and vice versa. There was little consistency to them, aside from the poor spelling. He'd told Donna how he missed her and loved her. In another, mistakenly sent to Julie, he accused her of still "fukng" her old boyfriend just after they'd gotten married. Then, ugly gibberish to Julie concerning the recently discovered activities with her new boyfriend. Disjointed and inarticulate threats to withhold the purchase of a car for her sixteenth birthday. In another, meant for his wife, he let her know what a "spoiled can't" their daughter was becoming under her watch. Growing weary, Ray closed his messages.

He set down the phone and went to the restroom. The overwhelming odor of urine penetrated his blood-caked nostrils. It was splattered all over the wall, toilet, and floor. After a lengthy emptying of his bladder, he checked his appearance in the medicine cabinet mirror. Both eyes were encircled in purplish bruises. He spent a few minutes trying to clean up his face and nose.

On the back porch, Ray stood looking over the lake, still feeling drunk. His mind began to play games. Phrases from the online real estate ad ran on an endless reel: unique find, 1.5 acres, boat dock, wooded, secluded, lakefront, tucked away, gentle slope, waterfront, cul-de-sac, gorgeous, sanctuary, water access…

Then the lyrics of the Chris Stapleton song began. The same segments, over and over and over.

Mercifully, the faint sound of the front doorbell interrupted the cycle.

Amen, Chris. I've done a whole lotta shit myself. But that someone I was, apparently, is somebody I still am.

He walked back through the house and opened the front door. Elise stood wearing her cowboy hat, arms folded across her chest. When she saw his battered face, hers filled with sympathy.

"It's you," Ray said.

"'Fraid so."

He stood looking at her for a moment, then surveyed the sky as if expecting black helicopters to come swarming down.

Elise followed his gaze. "It's just me. Can I come in?"

"Sorry." Ray stepped back and motioned her in.

She followed him into the parlor.

"Have a seat," he said. "I'll get us some waters."

Ray watched Elise give the room a careful inspection, then made for the kitchen.

"It's different," he heard her say. Then after a short pause. "Wild night?"

Ray entered the room carrying two plastic water bottles. He saw her eyeing the nude Polaroids that littered the floor.

"Don't... Listen, I found those in the attic. I was considering turning them over to the police. Your uncle said the guy's still practicing."

Elise picked a few off the floor and studied them. "Wouldn't do much good. They seem pretty enthusiastic about it. Aware of what they're doing. And they don't look underaged. And...I'd appreciate you letting me go through them before you do anything. I seem to recall taking off my own shirt a time or two for a script that wasn't yet due a refill, if you know what I mean."

Ray gave her a surprised glance.

She shot him a dimpled smile. "Soooo, yesterday I relapsed." She reached down and held up a little whiskey bottle. "Cute. They can't sell real bottles, but they can sell the gift boxes with these little tasters."

Ray looked confused.

"Smoky Cove Tavern gift shop? You take a little trip in your new boat last night?"

Ray frowned as it came back to him.

"Looks like we were of the same mind," she said. "Anyway, thankfully, someone called Les. Someone looking out for me. Somehow, I'd found my way to a little backyard gathering. And one drink led to another, which led to a few pills, which led to me dancing in the bed of a pickup with my tits out. A bunch of rednecks circled around, making fuck faces at me."

Ray looked even more surprised.

"So, Les did what Les does. He rescued me."

"I'm sorry," Ray said.

"No need to be." Elise tilted her head. "It *happens*, Ray. Not the end of the world."

"I saw you on the back of the bike," Ray said. "Thought the worst. Maybe...like, he'd drugged you. The... You were tied to him—"

"Yeah, I was a zombie and...Jimmy hitched me to Les, and they got me the hell outta there. Must have been a pretty sight to see. If you could, once again, please spare Uncle Bo the worry..."

"No, no," Ray said, shaking his head. "Not a word. I've done plenty worse."

"This used to be my favorite place in the world. Disneyland for grown-ups," she said, scanning the room. "Well, 'grown-up' might not describe..."

Ray scoffed. "Yeah, I'm not feeling at the peak of maturity this morning."

The familiar rumble of motorcycle engines assaulted his ears.

"I came over to see if I...I thought maybe I could introduce you to Les and the others?"

"And why do I want to meet Les and the others? I prefer my head attached to my body."

She shot him a quick glance.

"Yeah, I remember. Sobered up a little when the knife touched my face. Thanks for calling them off."

"Nobody was going to hurt you, Ray. They didn't know who you were, and...there's a couple of sick fucks around here that don't like that I'm trying to get clean. And others who I'm still...making *loan* payments to, you might say."

"Why were you in my little building up there that day?"

"Hiding. They know where Les lives, so... Like I said, you could have been anybody last night. Anyway, listen. Les is my sponsor. He's a recovering addict. He rides a big loud bike, but he's not a *biker*. He's a counselor, a respected mechanic, and a very loyal friend. There's a group of us. A couple of girls, mostly guys. And we're...tryin'. Helpin' each other. Got each other's back." Elise tilted her head toward the front doors. "So, whadaya say?"

"No thanks. I've done my time with whiners sharing their *stories* and whatnot."

"Oh? Let me guess, you don't share?"

"Why would I tell strangers? Why are they entitled to revel in my fucking misery?"

"C'mon. No one enjoys hearing... It sucks. It's hard. It takes balls to open up like that. So..." She smiled at him for a long moment. "Strap on a pair and come with me."

He stared at her dimples, her beautiful, tired eyes, her chapped lips, and thought of his daughter. After a moment, she looked away, and her smile faded as if surrendering to futility.

• • •

Four men, including Les, and one female sat in plastic chairs surrounding a crude fire pit filled with ashes and charred fragments of wood.

Ray and Elise took two empty chairs as the woman continued to speak unabated.

Ray's battered, multicolored face received reticent glances.

She finished and Les said, "Thank you, Jan. Thank you for coming and thank you for sharing today."

For the first time, Ray had a chance to see Les up close and in natural light. He was handsome, with dark hair beginning to gray at the temples. His dark, almond-shaped eyes were intense but caring. He was a big guy, but not heavy. He sat with his long legs splayed in front of him, his fingers interlocked on top of his head. A slight, continuous smile.

"Anyone else?" Les asked.

Heads lowered. Shoes kicked at gravel.

"All right," Les said, finally. "I got one." He sat up straight and put his hands on his knees. "Some of you've heard this, but we got some new folk here."

Elise gave Ray a quick, encouraging smile, then turned her attention back to Les.

"Senior in high school. Living in the *district* in Olivia. Dad's a CPA. Mom's a dental hygienist. Got the pretty girlfriend wearin' my letterman. Got the money, got the big lake house, got dad's boat. Richie Rich." He shook his head and smiled, then brushed something off the leg of his jeans. "Needless to say, I got friends.

"A beautiful Labor Day weekend. Parents are in Hilton Head. And my house is the place to be. We start drinking at ten in the morning. By early afternoon, you can imagine. Someone has the grand idea of taking the boat out. I know it's off limits, but no one's there to stop me.

"We pile on. Too many of us, too much weight. I take off and...not as aware as I should be. Not as diligent. Too fast. Lake's crowded that weekend, of course. And there's some good-sized boats out there. Anyway, I let a big roller catch us from the side. We flip. Multiple times. Only bright side is nobody died. Three hurt. And my friend Toby gets in a little scuffle with the propeller. Chews up his leg. And other body parts that I'll leave to your imagination.

"He still lives in Olivia. Successful guy. Commercial real estate. He's also a councilman or somethin' in the local government. I have the pleasure of running into him from time to time. He has a...prosthesis. You wouldn't know. Unless you knew. He's married and...two children. Adopted."

Les shook his head. "I stayed off the water after that. But not the booze. And not...*other* things." He pointed toward the front of the house. "That bike saved my life. When I got sober, that was my coping mechanism. My coping *machine*.

"So, I try to do some good. I got the pill mill shut down so Mr. Ray could move in."

There were smiles and glances. Ray grinned and nodded appreciatively.

"Don't take a rocket scientist to know that a respectable clinic isn't seeing patients at three in the morning. But, hey, at least I met this ugly thing here." Les pointed at Elise.

Elise gave a pageant wave.

"And now, she's met Ray. And Ray is here. Maybe the good Lord's doin' somethin'?"

During a break, they stretched their legs and walked around lighting cigarettes.

Elise was talking with the woman named Jan. Ray felt his phone vibrate and pulled it from his pocket. Julie.

"Hey, sweetie," Ray answered, trying to sound upbeat.

"Did you get drunk?" she asked flatly.

Ray inhaled. "Yeah. I blew it."

"Okay. Last night you—"

"Yeah, your mom told me. I'm sorry. Please just...delete them."

"What happened...did you..." She seemed to struggle for the words. "Did you *kill* someone? Is that why you and mom...?"

Obviously, he'd not performed an exhaustive review of the drunken texts from the previous night. He closed his eyes and recalled being back at the office in Nashville that following morning. His colleagues were watching the horrific on-the-scene news footage on the breakroom television. In the background, responders stood around two white sheets on a grassy bank beyond the overpass. In the foreground, the mangled, overturned white Mustang, its wide, rear tire still spinning.

"Okay, guys," Les called out. "Wanna wrap it up?"

"Can I call you back, sweetie? Julie?" Ray ended the call. He felt as if his very soul had dissolved.

They each retook their seats. "You okay?" Elise asked Ray.

Ray stared at the fire pit, his eyes wide and anxious.

"Hey," Elise whispered, playfully punching his arm.

"Anyone else got one for us before we say adios?" Les asked, scanning faces.

Ray sat doubled over in his chair, still staring into the ashes.

After a moment, Les said, "Okay, you shall be free. Listen up. Don't forget the fish fry next—"

"Wait," Ray said. He straightened in his chair and ran both hands over his sore face.

"Yeah, Ray?" Les said.

Ray rubbed his palms on the legs of his shorts. He closed his eyes tight, his face twisting in anguish. Finally, he blew out a long breath and whispered, "I got one for ya."

SUNSET
MASQUERADE

A NEAT, DIAGONAL line of white powder bisected the montage of flags. The flags were arranged inside a flaming emblem. The emblem was encircled by a white border. This was the image which adorned the front cover of his copy of the *1982 World's Fair Official Guide Book*. He grinned at the universal *no* symbol his temporary white line created when added to the white circular outline. Through a rolled up ten-dollar bill, he erased the line in two sweeps, then shuddered involuntarily. A wet finger mopped up the remains, which he massaged into his gums.

Alan Thomas had decided he would argue no more with his wife over whether to attend the big party that night. In their bedroom, he had the last word. They *would* go.

"Sherry, the time to avoid members of the Cross family will come soon enough," he reasoned. "For now, we play nice with the boss."

"*Fuck* Finley Cross," she snapped, then took a long sip of her vodka martini.

He grinned. "Well now, his bookkeepers have a history of doing just that. Maybe he'd replace Marsha with you, and you'll end up in the big house on the lake like you've always wanted."

"That's very funny. Thank you." Sherry drained the glass,

43

wiped the bright red lipstick from its rim, and handed it to her husband.

"God, honey," Alan said, taking the glass. "Don't you see how it'll look if we don't show?"

"It would look like we were responsible, caring parents to our four-year-old child. We should be with our *daughter* on Halloween, instead of dressing up like assholes ourselves."

"You took her trick-or-treating. She got some candy, and she'll get a lot more with Michelle, later."

"Fifteen minutes around our complex is not what I'd call—"

"We're going to the goddamn party," Alan said.

He noticed she was wearing a black pants suit, one she'd often worn to work. "You're wearing that?"

Sherry looked in the mirror, then picked up the feathery stick mask off the vanity and held it to her face. "This is all I can muster. Sorry." She motioned with her free hand to the bed where lay a matching black mask, satin vest in a black-and-red diamond pattern, and a cheap black top hat. "There's yours."

"Why aren't you wearing that little dress?"

"I don't want to wear that little dress. I'm not eighteen years old."

"Oh. Okay. Well, I'm not sure I'm doing the masquerade thing. I found something else."

Sherry turned to him and lowered the mask, revealing a mixed expression of disbelief and curiosity.

With a sardonic smile, Alan had left the bedroom, set the martini glass on the banister, and made his way quietly up the carpeted stairs to his study on the top floor of their lakefront condominium. He locked the door behind him and began gathering his goodies.

Presently, he cleared the desk of evidence and locked away his stash. He stood by the window overlooking the lake and the long, neat line of boats berthed below. The doorbell rang. He could hear two muted voices. Michelle the babysitter, he reckoned.

Social events—particularly asinine ones, as in this case—were not Alan's thing. He was a numbers geek, awkward in social settings and forced conversation with imbeciles. This being closing day of the World's Fair, Finley's quick-witted, more refined, and enjoyable brother would be thirty miles away, mastering the ceremony of some big consummation blowout downtown. Thus, Alan would suffer the obnoxious sycophants of Finley's subaltern gathering sans his usual relief outlet.

The blow would increase his tolerance for the impending alcohol and bullshit, both of which were sure to flow in abundance.

He spun around at the sound of the doorknob being worked.

"Daddy," Sonya yelled from the other side of the door.

"Comin', baby." He walked to the door, turned the bolt, and opened it. "How did that get locked?" he wondered aloud. "That's so weird," he said, looking down at the human sunflower that was his daughter.

"You're so weird," she said, giggling.

He hoisted her up and held her in his arms. "Are you going to be okay while Mama and Daddy are away tonight?"

"Uh-huh," Sonya mumbled uncertainly.

"Michelle's fun, right? You like her? She's gonna take you to a neighborhood with a bunch of trick-or-treaters, and the people are rich, so you'll get lots of candy. Then, when you get back, you can keep your costume on and scare the ones that come to our door."

"Yeah, but sunflowers aren't scary. And anyway, there won't be no trick-or-treaters comin' way out here."

"Sure, there'll be," he said, easing her down. "Go on and show Michelle your costume. I better hurry and get mine on."

Sonya ran out of the study, and Alan went to the small couch where he'd thrown his last-minute costume replacement. He slipped its paper-thin bottoms over his khakis and the top over his Izod shirt. He positioned the little round hat on his head and grabbed the plastic handcuffs. Returning to the window, he grinned at his reflection while spinning the cuffs on his finger.

"Alan, let's go!" Sherry yelled from the bottom of the stairs. "I want to get back early."

Alan decided he could use another quick dose of tolerance.

Downstairs, he ignored the confused look from Michelle and took a knee in front of Sonya. "Everyone is going to think you are soooo pretty."

She smiled, looking him up and down. "Why are you—"

A horn blared. "I gotta go before Mama changes her mind." He stood and turned to Michelle. "You're good till midnight, maybe one?"

"That's fine," she said, her head nodding, eyes smiling.

"You girls have fun," Alan said, clasping plastic cuffs around each of his wrists. "If you need anything, the Suttons are at 127."

He stepped onto the front porch in his jailbird stripes. Squinting into the glare of the harvest gold Volvo sedan's headlights, he was sure he saw his wife's jaw drop. He shuffled to the passenger window and peered in. "You'll have to drive," he yelled, baring his restraints.

Sherry sped along the narrow, winding road that followed the lake until she reached the interstate. The couple was silent, Alan aloof, his wife fuming. As she veered onto the exit which led over the bridge to the town of Olivia, she said, "Take off those ridiculous cuffs."

Finley Cross's lake house was located on the north shore across from and about a mile downstream from Olivia's historic Old Town district. The much-fancied subdivision came into view as they crossed the bridge. Alan peered down at the water as a lone vessel made its way slowly up the channel, its lights glowing in the dusk. He rolled down his window and sent the toy restraints twirling into the air and over the bridge.

Sherry switched the position of her hands on the wheel, her face twitching with silent annoyance. Alan could coast through tense interludes for as long as was necessary, but he knew his wife was ready to combust.

"So, you'd actually move all the way out here?" he asked at last.

"Why not? Do you have something against raising our daughter in a safe, beautiful, historic town? Water is everywhere you look. You could boat around with your vodka and cigar hanging out of your mouth—"

"I do that now. Without having to navigate tree limbs and floating bags of garbage. Which, by the way, could cause me to spill my vodka."

"Lake Olivia is beautiful."

"It's not a lake, honey. Technically, it's a *reservoir*. You really should learn the history of your hometown. We could drive through on the way. There's a plaque—"

"Please shut up, Alan."

"They should have flooded the entire county." He glanced at his wife, her mouth tight and narrow. "Finn's home should be on the market soon. It's much grander than the condo, huh?"

"Much," she shot back. "And I wouldn't have to listen to our neighbors screwing on the other side of the wall."

Alan grinned and turned toward his window again. But he couldn't resist one last quip. "You'll know just the right time to start checking the real estate section."

The Crosses' property comprised a long and narrow piece of land that jutted out over the lake. The sprawling midcentury abode sat nestled in mature trees and well-manicured shrubbery. Its clean, angular lines integrated nicely with the impressive landscaping which, Alan was sure, Finley lifted nary a finger to upkeep.

Already, the street was lined with Town Cars, Continentals, Sevilles, and Eldorados, along with a sensible Toronado, a Grand Marquis, and a Jeep Wagoneer. Predictably, Finley's beloved mint-condition 1960 Porsche 356 convertible was on display in the driveway. Alan noticed several gawkers had encircled it as Sherry eased by looking for a place to park.

"Don't they ever tire of spewing adulations at that fucking car?" Alan wondered aloud. "I mean, it's right there, every party. Same guests, every party."

His wife ignored him and pulled in front of a late model BMW. She cut the ignition and sat silently.

Alan lifted her mask by its stick off the dashboard and began waving it at her. "Don't forget this."

"Alan..." she began, then stopped. She took the mask, studied it, then turned to her husband. "Please try to understand how hard this is for..." Her eyes narrowed and her mouth widened. "This man has destroyed my... *Our*..." She lifted the mask to her face. A single tear ran beneath it and came to a rest on the tip of her chin.

"Let's not be *too* chastising, darling. We each played our little roles." He was about to reach over to wipe her tear but was distracted by a white van pulling partway into the Crosses' driveway. He shook his head at the rudimentary insignia of Olivia's venerated Smoky Cove Tavern affixed to its side. "Oh, good. Catering's here. Fried finger foods," Alan said. "If corruption don't do 'em in, cholesterol surely will."

Sherry whispered, "Can we *please* get this over with?" as she wiped her face with the back of her hand.

"Sorry," Alan said regretfully.

They were able to pass the Porsche admirers with Alan offering an all-encompassing "hello" and "good to see you." He followed his wife down the pathway laid with gigantic flat stones leading to the back of the house. Habitually, the bulk of the night's debauchery would take place on the outside patio and in the spacious ground-floor rec room.

As they approached the patio, Finley's third wife, Marsha, twenty-two years his junior, hurried over to greet them. Cleavage spilled out of her Playboy Bunny getup. The two women hugged and kissed cheeks. Alan suddenly felt a bit jumpy, agitated. He wished he'd curtailed his pre-party activities back at the condo. He needed a drink.

After his own bosomy hug with their cohost, Alan said, "Thanks for having us, Marsha," and disappeared into the house through the sliding glass doors. He could only imagine the expression he'd left on his abandoned wife's face.

The two women had a delicate relationship, Sherry being Marsha's replacement as Finley's bookkeeper and Marsha being all too privy to her husband's philandering.

Inside was an impressive wet bar fashioned after an authentic Irish pub, with a brushed stainless steel footrail, hand-rubbed maple woodwork, and a double tap built-in kegerator. Alan nodded to the hired bartender, who was dressed as an old-fashioned saloon barkeep, complete with white button-down shirt, red-and-white striped vest, arm garters, a long white apron, and a handlebar mustache that, upon closer critique, appeared authentic. He looked Alan up and down. "Bet yer plenty thirsty after the escape. Name yer poison."

Alan bellied up and put a foot on the rail, "Whatcha offerin'?"

The bartender gave a wide, toothy smile. "We got—"

Merle Haggard's "I Think I'll Just Stay Here and Drink" blasted from the back of the room. The two men turned to see Finley Cross's hulking figure hovered over his prized 1952 Wurlitzer jukebox along the back wall, just beyond the pool table.

"Gonna be a long goddamn night," Alan said from the side of his mouth. "I may go back...turn myself in."

The bartender smiled again and continued a little more loudly, "We got pretty much whatever you want. Mixers. Jack, Jim, Smirnoff, Canadian Clu—"

"What's on tap?" Alan asked.

"Tap's dry," the bartender said, shaking his head. He moved down the bar a few feet and gestured to a neat row of nine single cans of World's Fair Beer of assorted colors. "Cross bought enough to last a decade."

Alan rolled his eyes. "Vodka and soda. With a lime, please."

The bartender held out his hand. "Ethan."

"Alan Thomas. Pleasure."

Alan was promptly served and took a sip of his drink. He scanned the adorned crowd, looking for his wife. She was nowhere that he could see, but, he did lock eyes with Don Corleone. Maynard Kell, board chairman at the bank where Alan served as chief loan officer, was walking toward him in a black tuxedo with a red rose pinned to its lapel, a black bow tie, and a bullet-riddled, blood-splattered white dress shirt. His normally wavy, jet-black hair was slicked straight back with spray-on gray added above his ears.

Alan greeted him with a slow bow. "Godfather."

"Looks as if you've gotten yourself into some, ah...trouble," Maynard said, borrowing Brando's slow, raspy delivery. He lowered his head to sniff the artificial flower under his chin. Then, looking around the chaotic room, asked, "What can I do for you on this beautiful evening?"

"Have one of your associates put me out of my misery?" Alan said and took another sip of his drink.

Maynard laughed, then straightened his face and resumed character. "That I cannot do. Look," he said, his eyes darting around the room, "I do believe this drug business is gonna destroy us in the years to come..." He reached inside his tux and flashed a small Ziploc bag. "But for now...?"

Alan nodded affirmatively, sipping his drink through a tiny straw.

"Shall we let our gracious host in on—"

The men flinched at the loud crack of colliding billiard balls.

"Who's got the balls to take me on?" Finley Cross stood at the far end of the custom Olhausen. "No pun intended, of course." He wore a dark-red, black-trimmed smoking jacket, silky black pajama bottoms, and corduroy house slippers. A pipe hung from his plump red lips.

"Hello, Finn," Alan said.

Maynard shook his head. "Hef's done took me for twenty dollars this evening. Besides..." He patted his jacket and addressed Hefner directly, "I have something that might interest you more." Then he raised his chin and declared in Brando fashion, "I'm a man who knows how to return a favor."

"It is I who is in debt to you, Don Corleone," Finley said. "Let's just say your *flexibility* over recent months is greatly appreciated." Then, turning to Alan, "Both of you, seriously. My brother asked me to pass that along. But, yeah, I believe I can slip away for a moment."

"To the smoking room?" Maynard suggested.

"Indeed," Finley replied, gesturing toward a closed door in the back corner of the rec room.

Alan checked again for his wife. Nowhere.

"Sherry told me yous both doin' the Mardi Gras masquerade thing," Finley said. "What the hell's with the prison garb?"

"Oh, that other getup just didn't feel right," Alan said flippantly. Then thought, *Get a good, long look, Bubba.*

Finley ushered his guests into the smoking room, which doubled as a home office. Then, he stepped inside and locked the door behind him. As he turned back to face the room, Maynard was waving the baggy at him. "Do the honors, Hef?"

The walls of the dimly lit room were covered with gaudy black-and-gold floral wallpaper above dark wood paneling. The men sat in cushioned leather chairs around a circular glass top table. Finley arranged three neat lines on a tray that had held a crystal decanter set, a gift from a previous wife.

Each man consumed his third and leaned back in his chair waiting for the effects to take hold.

"Oh, Alan," Finley said, snuffling. He pinched his nose a few times, then began arranging the decanter set back onto the tray in the center of the table. "I'm gonna need somethin' pushed through pretty quick. Old family friend..." Finley leaned toward board chairman Maynard Kell and whispered, "You ain't hearin' this."

"Hell, I can't hear nothin' over my damned heart poundin.'"

Finley laughed, his face flush from the drugs and hypertension. Turning back to Alan, he asked, "You'll be in the office tomorrow?"

"I will," Alan confirmed. "Physically, at least." He blinked his eyes and shook his head quickly.

Maynard grinned. "Potent, huh? That's from my guy in Miami."

Finley continued, "Development deal for a subdivision. This one over in Scarsburg. Name is Evergreen Corp. Collateral's gonna look good." He winked. "Just don't get too concerned with the facts."

"Evergreen. I'll take care of it," Alan said. He looked over at Maynard, who was now standing on one end of a strip of green artificial turf working his grip on a putter he'd lifted from a golf bag resting in the corner. "You still deaf, Mr. Chairman?"

Maynard gave a quick smile as his downturned head repeatedly moved from the ball at his feet to the hole on the opposite end, his expression tight with concentration.

Alan continued more quietly, "We got a hell of a lot on the books with this fair, Finn."

"Don't I know it." Finley laughed. "The city'll be digging

its way outta this for the next twenty-five years. We'll move it somewhere else once it's signed."

Alan began shaking his head.

Finley held up a hand and nodded. "Listen, Al," he said, rubbing his fingers together. "Lock it in, and you'll be well taken care of. Hell…might end up with enough to trade in the ol' mustard monstrosity for somethin' more, uh…attractive. Hey, did you get a look at my 356 in the driveway?"

Alan ignored the question and slapped Finley's knee. "I'll be there bright and early, stamp inked and ready." Then, knowing full well this particular sham of a loan would never be executed, he decided to have a little fun with his boss. "But do me a favor. When I get into that paperwork, I don't wanna see Sherry's signature as Secretary or—"

"Nah, nah," Finley said, taken aback. "All real players, all of 'em in the business, in one way or another." He leaned closer to Alan. "Listen, I'm sorry Sherry's gettin' hassled. It'll go away. They like to stick their big noses in the door every so often to let us know they're still breathin'. And any legal fees, taken care of. That's a given."

Well, they buy everything else, Alan thought. *Why not silence.*

"Speaking of…" Alan stood. "I'd better check on my wife."

"I saw her earlier cluckin' with Marsha," Finley said, springing up from his chair.

"Fuuuck, yeah!" Maynard blurted out as a golf ball dropped into the hole. "All right, Finn, I need a chance to win back my dough. Twenty on the next shot?"

Alan left the room without closing the door behind him. He made his way through the crowd, which had become a bit more spirited during the men's brief business meeting. He found Sherry outside on the patio talking, not to Marsha but to Erin Brownlee.

Erin, along with her husband, Bear, owned the Smoky Cove Tavern and Marina in downtown Olivia. Alan reckoned the old friends were catching up. The food had been laid out on two long folding tables covered with black tablecloths and the vultures were already picking at it. He walked over to Sherry and Erin, smiled, but said nothing. From the jukebox, Johnny Cash began singing "25 Minutes to Go" to a captive audience at Folsom Prison. The song's lyrics count down the final twenty-five minutes before a prisoner's rendezvous with the gallows. Alan looked at Sherry and said, "Honey, it's my theme song." He began clogging awkwardly to the upbeat number in his ill-fitting prison outfit.

Sherry watched her husband with a mix of embarrassment and disgust. She studied his face suspiciously, then asked, "Uh...Alan, dear, you remember Erin from the tavern?"

"I do," he said, his movements temporarily calmed. Then he feverishly wagged his finger in Erin's face. "Uh... Oh..." He searched his mind before blurting out louder than necessary, "Award-winning fried bologna sandwich, right?"

Sherry slapped his hand away from Erin's face and looked at him in disbelief. "Why don't you use that energy to get us a drink. Erin, a quick one before you hit the road?"

"No, sweetie, thank you," Erin said. "I better get back before Bear lets the place burn down. Last time I left the baby with him, I returned to find her dancing on top of the bar." She rolled her eyes.

"Sweet Bethany. She's good?" Sherry asked.

"She's gr—"

"One drink," Alan said, starting to move his body again. "Have one drink with us."

"I'd love to, but I can't."

"I'll take a beer, *please*, Alan," Sherry said, her annoyance obvious.

"What color?" he asked.

Sherry shook her head, perplexed.

"Never mind." Alan danced across the patio and disappeared into the house.

The Man in Black's electrified version of the disjointed folk song had whipped the Halloween revelers into a frenzy. Alan made his way to the bar, circumventing the outer layer of folks standing around watching and laughing and pointing at an inner circle of alcohol-infused fools dancing and singing and hollering and knocking into one another.

Bartender Ethan pointed as Alan approached. "Vodka, soda, lime."

"Double vodka straight," Alan replied.

With only eighteen minutes to go, Johnny Cash was laughing in the sheriff's face and spitting in his eye.

Alan said, "Oh, and my wife wants a beer. Which color do you recommend?"

Ethan smiled. "How about *big orange*?"

"Well, of course."

Ethan poured a generous ration of Smirnoff into a clear plastic cup. "Wouldn't have taken you for a country music fan," he said, scooting it toward his convict customer who was moving his head to the music.

Alan turned to Ethan. "This one hits home." He drained the cup in two quick gulps.

Ethan flashed his wide, white grin, then spun around and retrieved an orange World's Fair Beer can from the fridge behind him. When he turned back around, Alan was tapping a finger on the rim of the empty cup. Ethan sat the can on the bar and ripped off its tab. "Another double?"

Alan nodded, then said, "Wait, gimme your hand."

Ethan held out his hand as if to shake. Instead, Alan visually sized it up. "Three fingers, barkeep."

"Of course, sir," Ethan said straight-faced.

Alan drained it as hastily as its predecessor and said, "Another, please, kind sir." He turned to watch the scene, anticipation mounting toward that inevitable final minute.

Johnny had nine more to go as he awaited the pardon. There'd be no pardon for Alan, but he'd been assured minimum security. The FDIC clown even mocked the country club-like atmosphere most white-collar offenders like Alan could expect to inhabit. Although with the conviction, there would be no subsequent career in the finance game.

Sherry's open beer can sat sweating on the bar. "Another, please," Alan said. "The wife's driving. Plus, I've only got..." Alan felt himself souring to the tune as Johnny arrived at that final minute, presently seeing buzzards and hearing crows.

On cue, a drunken chorus joined Johnny. "One more minute to go!"

As the doomed prisoner swung to his death, there were raucous cheers and hoots and hollers. Alan's face twisted into a scowl. Seconds later, Lynn Anderson launched into her rendition of "Rocky Top" and a roar of affirmation followed. Alan, his back against the bar, tossed down vodka while observing the revelers with repugnance.

He spotted Finley Cross, ever the distinguished host, skipping around in a circle on a single wooden crutch he'd gotten from God knows where. Everyone clapped and stomped along, allowing him plenty of room for his display of inebriated buffoonery. Hearty laughs and squeals erupted when the belt of his smoking jacket came loose, exposing his floppy, hairless man breasts. Alan gave Ethan a look. The bartender stood on his tiptoes to gain a better view of the spectacle.

Scattered throughout the rec room were several weight-bearing steel support poles, the bottom half of each wrapped in three-quarter-inch nautical rope. There came a unified "Whoa" from the crowd. Then another, longer, "Whooooa." Alan stepped onto the bar's footrail, just in time to witness an off-balance Finley Cross stumbling forward for what seemed like an eternity. One of his Hugh Hefner slippers flew into the air, and above all the yelling and the music, Alan heard the crack of the wooden crutch breaking in two, followed by the low, echoing thud of Finley's skull connecting with one of the roped poles.

"Oooh," came the chorus, followed by a rush of aid from concerned guests.

Alan hopped off the rail and held up his empty cup. Ethan returned to his normal height as well and reached for the Smirnoff.

Through the frantic milling around of those trying to help an injured and humiliated Hef, Alan noticed Sherry standing, arms crossed, at the sliding glass doors.

• • •

The party never regained its momentum after Finley's misadventure, and most everyone had gone home by the time Erin Brownlee returned in the midnight aftermath to break down and pack up her belongings. Sherry helped her load everything into the tavern's van, then the two sat at a wrought iron table on the patio to talk.

"Never a dull moment at a Cross shindig," Erin said. "Last

time they had us cater was their big Fourth of July party. You weren't here?"

"Thankfully, no." Sherry sighed. "We'd taken Sonya to Destin."

"Let me tell you what you missed. When I came back to gather up my things, there were about ten of 'em in the hot tub." She nodded at the Jacuzzi sitting quiet and covered against the house. "It was bubblin', and they were rowdy, but I wasn't payin' them any mind. I start clearing the tables and boxing things up when I hear wet footsteps against the tile here. I look over, and some old bald guy is stompin' across the patio buck naked, goes down the yard and ducks behind a tree. I tried to be inconspicuous as I watched him high-step it back up through the grass, his peter floppin' up and down, a big smile on his face as the others hollered and whistled."

"Oh. My. God," Sherry said wide-eyed.

"Yeah," Erin assured her. "Oh, honey, that was nothin'. Few minutes later, I hear some women cackling, and a man says, 'Look. Hey, look. It's me in my high school portrait.' Overcome with curiosity, I glance over to see a naked gal, legs spread wide, squatting over the old streaker perv, who is just sitting in the hot tub with a goofy smile on his face. Her...uh...pubic hair is resting on the top of his bald head. Looks like he's got a big red...*fro*."

The ladies shared a hearty laugh.

Alan came through the sliding doors and joined them.

"How is the old fool?" Erin asked.

"Embarrassed, I believe."

"Why, whatever does he have to be embarrassed of?" Sherry pondered aloud. "Where's bunny boobs Marsha?"

"Fuming," Alan said. "She doctored him up, then barricaded herself in the master suite." Alan clamped his hands together. "I've thanked her on behalf of the both of us for a lovely evening. No need for you to bother."

"And what have *you* been doing, dear?" Sherry asked.

"Just…" Alan looked around at the near vacant patio, his body swaying back and forth.

"I believe I've had enough merriment," Sherry told her husband. Then promised Erin, "I'll come see you at the tavern, soon."

The Thomases did not speak on the drive home. Alan eventually slumped over in the passenger seat and fell asleep. He snored softly, his head occasionally thumping against the window.

• • •

"I can't believe I'm sending my own husband to prison." Sherry had said through tears as they drove home after meeting with attorneys.

"My *own* actions are…" Alan reminded her. "Your guy is smart, hon. Full immunity. There was no other play. He was right, we have to think of Sonya."

That was a lifetime ago. Subsequently, things seemed to have moved in slow motion, allowing for tensions to build and, for Alan, a growing sense of dread to pervade his psyche.

Presently, Monday, November 1, the morning after Finley's abridged jamboree, Alan was standing at the glass wall of his office watching cleanup crews mill around the fairgrounds. They seemed like tiny ants from his vantage point within the city's tallest building. He studied the 266-foot-high hexagonal steel truss structure crowned with a 75-foot gold glass sphere. *The great golden dome*, he thought. After all else is broken down and hauled away, as he himself would soon be, that will be the remnant. The reminder. In that moment, all his rage shifted to the inanimate ball that had sucked him in, jostled him around, and would eventually spit him out behind a very tall chain-link fence topped with concertina wire. *All that glitters...*

He attempted to justify his actions. Greed? Maybe. A little. But hell, it was a result of the perfect storm. Sherry's applying pressure, wanting a bigger place, preferably in Olivia. Then, of all fucking things, the World's Fair comes to town and every hustler and his incontinent grandmother needs quick cash to get in on it—none more lecherous than the bumpkin brothers themselves and their "inner circle" of friends and family. APPROVED. APPROVED. APPROVED. And just like that, the surreptitious manila envelopes begin appearing, accompanied by a wink and a slap on the back.

But the essential element, the wildcard; he'd become listless. *Apathetic.* Yes, that might be the word. In the whirlwind of multi-million-dollar hide the money games, locked-door snort fests, thousand-dollar table tabs at Regas and the Half Shell, and the occasional lap dance at the titty bar out on US 129, apathetic Al's existence gets a renewed dose of excitement...a dash of drama.

Sherry's absolute cooperation had certainly benefitted him. The mother of his child would serve no time for signing her name to whatever document Finley Cross had shoved under her cute little freckled nose. And his own sentence was reduced substantially. Still, Alan's stomach sank, and his scrotum tightened, when he allowed himself to ponder fifty-two months in prison on a medley of fraud charges. He hoped enough resolve would come in knowing the Cross brothers and all their arrogant cronies would get their comeuppance.

Bye-bye yacht, bye-bye Rolls, helicopter taxis. If only he could be there to watch Finley's beloved Porsche 356 get hauled away.

Alan walked to his desk and kicked up his feet. From a side drawer, he removed a bottle of Visine and applied several drops in each eye. Just before 10:00 a.m., Finley appeared in the doorway looking worse for wear. Rather than his usual three-piece, he wore khakis and a royal-blue golf shirt. In place of his polished wingtips, he sported well-worn docksiders. He also wore a purple-and-black bruise around his right eye and a Band-Aid just above it.

"The boys from Evergreen'll be here 'round two. Call if you need me."

"Ten-four. I'll handle it," Alan conciliated.

Finley went thudding down the hall as the door eased closed.

Alan checked his watch. *Any second now.*

When his desk phone rang, Alan lifted the handset, pushed the blinking red button, then returned it to its cradle.

Scanning the Monday morning newspaper, he came across a photo of a sad-faced clown standing on the sparse fairgrounds, the Sunsphere towering in the background. Hanging from shoulder straps was a large hand-painted sign which read, "It's Over."

Three quick, firm knocks came on his office door. "Federal agents. Alan Thomas?"

As the door swung open, Alan smiled at the halftone image. *Indeed, it is.*

• • •

Alan didn't sleep a wink the night before he was to turn himself in. He chose instead to treat his system with intermittent doses of blow and alcohol while, fittingly, a nasty storm tore through the region. Utterly despondent, Sherry had taken Valium and was out by 9:00 p.m.

At one point during the night, Alan stumbled into his daughter's room. He fell back onto the edge of her bed and stared down at her face, partially illuminated by a Tinker Bell nightlight. He kissed Sonya on the head, smelling her hair. He lifted her soft, tiny hand and studied it, squeezed it, then quietly left the room.

In his study, he took a piece of bank stationery from his desk drawer and made several attempts at a cordial letter to Sherry. Ultimately, he gave up and dashed off some instructions on how to access certain assets she was not aware existed and placed it in the drawer.

Sherry awoke groggy and hot. She turned to find Sonya pressed against her back. She hadn't even noticed her sneak into the bed during the night. She got to her feet and pulled at the damp nightshirt, fanning her clammy skin. Leaving Sonya sleeping soundly, she eased the bedroom door closed and shuffled her way to the kitchen.

By the time the carafe had filled, her mind was sharp enough to recall what day it was. A sense of dread overwhelmed her. She checked her watch to see it was already 9:47 a.m. Cursing herself and the Valium, she climbed the stairs to the top floor and entered Alan's study. It was empty and quiet. She walked to the window and peered down at the dock. Seeing the water's littered surface, she remembered the sound of a storm just before falling asleep. She hoped the lines on Alan's boat had held tight. It surprised her that she could have such a mundane thought under the current circumstances.

She descended two flights of stairs to the garage. Just outside the raised door, Alan sat in a lawn chair staring out at the lake with a thick cigar in his mouth.

He removed the cigar and said without facing her, "When you get back this afternoon, check in my desk, there's some information. Don't deposit anything. Use it for...day-to-day..."

Sherry nodded absently at the back of his head.

"Did you hear me?" he asked, still gazing ahead.

"Your desk."

• • •

For over two hours they traveled in silence. Sherry, her mouth clenched, eyes set straight ahead, had her hands fixed at ten and two on the Volvo's big steering wheel. Alan heard her whimper a few times but avoided eye contact. He was unable to muster any pity for her. She was distraught, sure, but within a few hours, she would be back in the condo curled up with their daughter on the couch watching *Sesame Street* or reclined in the big whirlpool tub sipping on a vodka martini.

Finally, he asked, "What are you and Sonya going to do today?"

Sherry turned to her husband with an expression he could not categorize. He decided to keep his mouth shut for the remainder of the trip.

• • •

The processing of new inmates was every bit as debasing as he'd expected. Afterwards, he was escorted to the second floor of C Building. The guard was a gangly, sticklike figure with a narrow, shiny face behind mirrored sunglasses. He wore his shirt tucked tightly into crisp trousers, which were tucked into polished black boots. Alan, fitted in a light-blue jumpsuit of a much softer fabric than his jailbird costume, shuffled his canvas slip-ons down a long corridor lined with cells on the left. On the right, a wall of dingy windows allowed for a view of the presently empty courtyard, or "yard" as he would learn to call it.

"Fresh meat!" came the proclamation from one of his new cohabitants.

The guard gave a wide, menacing grin. "Behave, ladies," he called out. Then, giving Alan's arm a squeeze, said, "That's no way to welcome Alan into your home."

The use of his first name made Alan even more unnerved.

The guard stopped abruptly and opened an empty cell. He motioned its new occupant in and locked it as Alan sat on the narrow cot. Giving Alan another wide smile, he said, "Hell, listen to me talkin' manners when I ain't even properly introduced myself. Mel Stone. It will be my distinct pleasure to serve you. Now, it's not well known, but my father-in-law is the warden of this...uh, rehabilitation facility."

Alan's stomach contracted violently, and he darted toward the steel head and released a rush of alcohol and bile into the bowl.

"Oops," Stone said, then waved a hand in front of his face. "Wheeew, man. That's a ninety-proof spill."

Alan returned to the bed and sat down hard on the thin mattress. He began reading the vile scrawl on the painted cinder blocks of the opposite wall, hoping to discourage further dialogue from the guard.

"You *look* at me," Stone said.

Alan exhaled and slowly turned to him.

"Now, for most folks here, it ain't the worst place they could've wound up. But *you*? Well..." Stone scoffed.

He removed his sunglasses, folded them, and hung them from his collar. "Warden Beecher recently lost a good portion of his life's savings. Money that happened to reside in a not-too-insured financial establishment operated by a couple of *former* friends of his. Brothers. Now, this money...this money that is no longer accounted for? A good bit of it, over forty-five thousand to be a mite more specific, was to be a gift to his daughter, who is my wife, see, upon her thirtieth birthday. Buuut"—Stone looked down at the floor, shaking his head slowly—"that milestone just blew by. But, hey, we did receive some very nice CorningWare in its stead."

He lifted his head and glared at Alan. "Ya know, they say you don't miss what you never had. Well..."

Alan flinched when Stone's baton slammed against the metal bars, causing loose paint to rain onto the concrete floor.

"That's a plain ol' fuckin' *lie*."

Alan's head fell into his hands.

"Uh-uh," Stone's voice echoed. "You keep that head up, Al."

Alan listened as the sound of Stone's retreating footfalls faded under a swelling chorus of snide banter.

"Hear that, Al? Mr. Fraudster?" Stone hollered over the ruckus, then hooted, "Ooh-wee! These next four years..."

Alan's face remained hidden as tears fell into his palms.

"They gonna *fly* by."

IN THE
MISTY BLUE YONDER

CHAPTER

1

H E HAD THE driver's side window rolled down on his new, gold-colored 1969 Cadillac Eldorado. The air grew cooler as he elevated into the lush, green highlands of the Southern Appalachian Mountains. In his right hand was a crudely drawn map which, now that he was getting rather close, he referenced frequently.

The referral—required for nonmembers—had come from a colleague by the name of Ronald Newsome. Judge Newsome, who sat on the bench of the circuit court of the man's home county, was well known and respected within his jurisdiction, charitable with his substantial generational wealth.

Checking the map one last time, the man made a final turn which, as labeled, dead-ended at a long, curved, graveled parking area along the edge of a dark pine forest.

The elderly judge's hand had been shaky as he scrawled on the cocktail napkin, but the results were accurate. *Thank you, Your Honor.*

The man parked, took a few purposeful breaths, got out, and eased the door closed. He patted his wallet, thick with fifty- and hundred-dollar bills, as he made his way through a sea of other luxury vehicles.

Ahead was a rectangular building with wood-planked siding painted white. "There's an old logging train depot," the judge had told him. "You'll go there and give your name to the attendant. A vehicle will take you on up to the resort."

Walking toward the depot, he noticed a family of five waiting on the low porch outside the building. The parents were well dressed, as were their three children, who were bantering amongst themselves. Scattered about them were several pieces of light-blue hard-case luggage. The man nodded as he approached, climbed the steps, and stood some distance away.

Someone emerged from the building and limped over to greet him. "Afternoon." The short, gimpy man had a gravelly voice. "Who do we got here?"

"Wakefield, Winston," the man answered pleasantly.

The attendant stood no more than five feet tall. He moved in quick, jerky motions. His enormous bottom lip, bulging cheekbones, and tiny close-set pale eyes formed an unfortunate composite. His hair was reddish brown and frizzy, his race indeterminable. A loud dashiki shirt only added perplexity.

Standing with one leg erect, the other bowed, he said in a singsong voice, "Let us fiiind Misterrr Wakefield..." while scanning the clipboard cradled in one arm. A quick movement with a pencil seemed to finalize the process. He smiled and said, "I'm Gaspar."

A crackle came from the two-way radio strapped to his hip. Several staticky, unintelligible words followed, to which Gaspar replied, "Teeen-four."

A long two-toned utility vehicle pulled into the parking area, gravel crunching under its bulky tires. Gaspar gave the driver a nod and went to meet the three-door, green-and-white Chevy Suburban as it slowed to a stop. Its driver got out, leaving the door ajar, and hurried around the vehicle. He grabbed the clipboard from under Gaspar's arm and disappeared inside the depot. Gaspar opened the Suburban's hatch and raised its back window. He came around, opened the third door, and motioned to the family. Then he went up on the porch, grabbed several suitcases, and began loading them into the vehicle's rear storage space.

The man calling himself Winston Wakefield got in through the front passenger door. The mother and children filed noisily into the seat behind him. Gaspar appeared in the passenger doorway. He leaned in and said to the man, "Trav'lin' light, brother? No bags?"

"Uh, no," the man replied hesitantly. He'd not thought of bringing a bag and searched for a viable response.

An impish grin spread across Gaspar's glistening face. His eyes narrowed into slits, and he whispered, "That's cool. Not an overnight stay, huh?" He gave the man a knowing wink.

Gaspar turned quickly and nearly bumped into the father, who was approaching the passenger door. The man slid to the middle of the front bench seat. The father got in, closed the door, and turned to the man. "If you were hoping for a quiet drive up the mountain, I apologize in advance."

"No need," the man said, smiling. "I have three myself." A pang of guilt gripped him, which he quickly shook away.

On the raucous, yet mercifully brief, trip to the resort, the man calling himself Winston Wakefield allowed his mind's eye a quick vision of girls parading through a dark lounge in skimpy attire showing off their assets, men rendering verdicts with a point of a finger or a nod of the head. Like in movies he'd seen.

Gaspar parked the Suburban at the base of a long, carved stone stairway which led up to the hotel. He said to the father, "We got a kid that carries luggage up the steps for tips."

The father replied, "I got three back there that I don't gotta pay a cent."

Gaspar laughed, then cut the engine. He looked behind him and said, "Okay, party people. Ready to climb? Who's gonna make it to the top first?"

"I am," the mother answered with confidence. "You heard your daddy; you munchkins get to haul the luggage."

A chorus of dissent followed.

Gaspar chuckled. "I dig that. The kiddos gotta earn their stay."

The father got out and opened the back door for his family. As Gaspar began unloading blue suitcases, a stocky young boy hurried over to help. Gaspar waved him away, saying, "They got this, Gere. I guess you're done for the day, little man. Try not to get eaten on the way home."

The boy grinned. "I'll try," he promised. "Night, Gaspar."

"Be here early in the morning," Gaspar said, wagging a stubby finger. "Tomorrow's a big day."

As the boy took off toward the blackness of the woods, Gaspar hollered after him, "Snakes! Boar! And bears!" He turned and grabbed the last two cases. "Oh, my!" he squealed, then let out a low chuckle.

The man calling himself Winston Wakefield got out last, walked to the foot of the stone steps, and stood a moment staring back at the excited family chattering loudly. He figured by now his own wife and kids would have landed in Tulsa, where his in-laws were surely waiting anxiously to begin the long holiday weekend with their daughter and only grandchildren. Again, he pushed the thought away, turned, and began the long climb up the steps.

CHAPTER

2

I'M FUCKIN' HURRRRTIN' right now, girl," Bryce Daniels whined into his iPhone.

"Oh, baby, I'm so sorry," Katie said, giggling. "You need a big, greasy breakfast."

"I know. And don't laugh, it's your fault."

"Hmm. I don't remember prying your mouth open and pouring Crown and Coke down your throat all night."

He let out a slow, painful moan. "You *must* have. I couldn't have done this to myself."

"Oh, but you did," she replied. "Chocolate milk. Drink lots of chocolate milk."

He was speeding down a rural two-lane highway on the opposite end of Myer County from his parents' home within the town of Olivia's historic district. Spotting a sign welcoming him to Whispering Winds Marina, and, less emphatically, the Rusty Anchor Restaurant, he slowed the new Ford F-150 Raptor—a gift from his parents for their class of 2019 high-school graduate—then turned onto a narrow road. To his left was a trailer park, to his right, farmland with a two-story white house and dilapidated barn. He turned at a second marina sign, eased down a short slope, veered to the right, and parked in front of a gigantic steel building painted royal blue. Ten minutes early, he waited with the engine running, the AC blowing in his face.

Katie's voice returned in his ear, "You remember makin' plans for tonight?"

"Uh…" He closed his eyes and thought. "I do, actually. Garrett's meeting us at my house. We're taking the boat to the tavern to watch the fight."

"Yay, Bryce. You're gonna be okay." Katie giggled again. "What time and I'll text Garrett?"

"Well, depends on how long 'spend the day with a geezer' takes."

"Bryce."

"What?"

"Be sweet. You might enjoy it. Although, my sister did it last summer. She got stuck with this old woman who refused to leave her house, so they just sat there while she yakked on and on about gardening. When to plant this, when to pick that. How to check if a cantaloupe is ripe…"

Bryce scoffed. "Oh, Lord. I can't wait."

"It did get interesting when she got to the part of pulling her Springfield twenty-two on the racoons to keep 'em away."

"Yep. That's interesting," he said dryly. "Guns and gardening."

"Well, it's good for your résumé."

"Yeah, you said that."

"Yeah, and I just said it again. So, what's the deal with your guy?"

"Kind of a bummer. They said he has, like, late-stage stomach cancer. That it's spread to his liver, maybe his brain."

"Oh, poor guy. Be really nice to him, Bryce."

"I will. It's just for a few days until his regular 'companion carer' is back. That's what they call 'em. I was told mentally he's fine, but his body's givin' in."

"Well, that's sad," Katie said.

"He's a liveaboard."

"Yeah? I didn't know that was legal anymore. That's right up your alley. Maybe he'll take you out on a voyage."

"I doubt it," Bryce said. "In his condition, I think that ship has sailed."

"Can you hear my eyes rolling? So, what time do you want me to tell Garrett to be at your house?" Katie asked. "You never answered me."

"Six okay? Fight's not till eight. That'll give us some time to partake."

"Fine," Katie said. "When do your parents get back from Buenos Aires?"

"Flight arrives late Tuesday night." Bryce caught a man's reflection in his side mirror. "Hey, I gotta go."

"Okay, babe, love you. Have fun."

"Yeah, right." He ended the call and checked his mirror again. The man was standing at the rear of the truck, waiting. Bryce killed the engine and opened the door. He stepped onto the footrail and nodded.

"Mornin'," the man said, coming toward him with his hand out.

"Hi." Bryce hopped down and shut the door.

They shook.

"Bo Shula. One of the owners here. Harbormaster."

"I'm Bryce. Here for Mr. McNabb. I'm fillin' in for Martha."

"Marta."

"*Marta*, sorry."

"Yeah, she told me there'd be someone taking her spot for a few days. Good to meet you, Bryce." Bo nodded toward the docks, where boats of varying shapes and sizes sat motionless in their slips. "His's over on the end."

"Hell," Bryce said, eyeing the decrepit vessel. "I don't have to get *on* that thing, do I? Will it even hold the weight of two bodies?"

"It will," Bo assured him with a grin. "I can testify."

They walked down the paved parking lot and onto the dock. Passing the Rusty Anchor Restaurant on their left, Bryce noticed a few early risers breakfasting alfresco on its deck. To their right, in the distance, was the marina office and fuel dock. Beyond that was a picturesque cove leading downstream to the main channel.

Midway to the slips, they stopped at a locked gate where Bo punched in some numbers on a keypad. There was a click, then he pushed open the gate and motioned Bryce through.

"Her name's *Betsy*," Bo said as they walked. "I don't know why. It wasn't his wife's name, he never married. Doesn't have kids. Marta couldn't get an answer from him, maybe you'll have more luck." He snickered. "Anyway, she's been berthed here 'bout three years now. McNabb had her up at Smoky Cove, but they'd been wranglin' with him to get her outta there."

"Oh, yeah," Bryce said. "Now I remember seeing her there."

Bo nodded. "I heard there was a hubbub, so I called Bear Brownlee. It seemed McNabb had stopped paying the slip fee after it increased. Minimally."

"Yeah, Bear and Erin, I know them. My parents live on this side of the peninsula...where the Ambrose house is. When we were kids, we used to swim to the tavern from my house and eat chili cheese fries on the back deck."

"Yeah? Good food up there. But we got 'em beat." Bo grinned. "Anyway, it took us a while to get *Betsy* to turn over, but we got her goin', barely. Late October just before the water level dropped. She coughed and sneezed the whole way here. Left a long, oily residue in her wake. Must've killed ten thousand fish in just those few miles."

Bryce smiled. "Has he had her out since?"

"Oh, no. Just sits here. He pays her slip fees, which are fifty bucks less than up there. When her captain goes, I'll have to have her towed outta here."

"How old is Mr. McNabb?"

"Well, the license I copied when I did his paperwork was over a decade expired. But it had a DOB of 1957."

"Hell," Bryce said. "He's not much older than my dad."

"Yeah, well, he'll look it. When you replace your medicinal treatment for stage four cancer with booze and Cohibas...it ages you."

At the end of the dock, Gerald McNabb's thirty-eight-foot sixties model Chris-Craft Sea Skiff sat still and foreboding. They turned and walked down the finger along the starboard side of the vessel. Bo ran his hand under the bow rail, snapping spiderwebs loose and wiping them on the back of his shorts.

As they came astern, Bo yelled, "Mr. McNabb. Got company."

Bryce peered through the screened enclosure of the cockpit. It was filled with cardboard boxes, piles of clothing, crushed beer cans, and stacks of magazines, newspapers, and books, some several feet high. On the aft deck stood a plastic table and two chairs. The table was littered with more empty beer cans and a circular tin container brimming with cigar butts buried in ashes. Several rod-and-reels lay in a tangled heap on the deck against the portside gunwale covered in a thick mesh of webs.

They heard loud, animated banter, and turned to see a

group of three young men idling by in a red-and-white 190 SSi. It was similar to Bryce's dad's, but several model years older. He suddenly became eager to get his little do-gooder assignment over with.

Bo yelled again, "Mr. McNabb, you got company."

Gerald McNabb appeared at the screen door with what looked to be a folded magazine or newspaper clamped under his arm.

"There he is," Bo said enthusiastically.

The old man slid open the screen door, stepped through, turned, and closed it. He wore an unbuttoned threadbare pale-green guayabera shirt, with black-framed eyeglasses sticking out the breast pocket. His stained khaki cutoffs hung to his knees. A shock of yellowish-white hair spilled out from under a new-looking light-blue baseball cap boasting the Rusty Anchor Restaurant logo, which Bryce found comical but wasn't sure why.

McNabb circumvented the ladder that led up to the flybridge, shuffling his ragged sandals across the wood-planked deck. Bryce grimaced at the long, brownish toenails. It wasn't until he reached the starboard gunwale that McNabb at last raised his head to the men. His jaundiced eyes went from Bo to Bryce and back to Bo.

"Mr. McNabb, this is Bryce. Bryce, Gerald McNabb."

McNabb looked at Bryce, then to Bo Shula again.

"You remember Marta has a few days off? Bryce'll be takin' her place till she gets back from vacation on Wednesday. Still up to you what you do and where you go...as long as Bryce agrees to it, and y'all call in and let them know where you are and when you plan on returning."

Gerald McNabb began climbing out of the vessel, ignoring Bryce's extended hand.

Bo grinned at Bryce knowingly.

"You thinkin' maybe the flea market?" Bo asked. "It's Saturday."

McNabb stepped heavily onto the dock. "I'm aware of what day of the week it is, thank you."

Bryce gave Bo a look. Bo tried again, "Maybe y'all could take a trip up the highway to the antique shops?"

"I'll wait for Marta to get back," McNabb said in a croaky voice and began walking away.

"Wait'll you see the fancy truck Bryce has," Bo called after him.

"Just wanna eat breakfast."

"C'mon," Bo said to Bryce. "He'll warm up after we get some food in him."

As they followed at a distance, Bryce whispered, "So, do you have to handle all his...care?"

"Yeah, well, he's chosen to discontinue treatment. He won't say it, but I think he wants to be aboard *Betsy* when his time comes. Wants to be surrounded by his...*stuff*." Bo chuckled. "Be able to smoke his cigars and drink his hooch."

"Can't blame him," Bryce said. "Goin' out on his own terms."

"I'm sure Marta briefed you on what you can expect?"

Bryce nodded. "Yeah. Nothing out of the ordinary for someone at his stage...in his condition. Falling asleep midsentence. Lack of appetite—"

"Oh, he'll order enough to feed a village," Bo chimed in. "Just won't eat much of it. Marta said lately he's been looking back some. Reminiscing."

"That part's easy," Bryce said. "I just sit there and listen."

Bo scoffed. "Few weeks ago, he burst into the office down there, said he'd seen his 'mama.' He was sure she'd come aboard *Betsy* and that she spoke to him. Marta had warned us of this kinda thing. Some of the behaviors to watch for, peculiarities to expect. Anyway, I guess out of sheer curiosity, my niece, Elise, tracked down his mother, Zoe Ruth McNabb. Or rather her obituary on a Wyoming newspaper's website.

"Never known him to have any friends. If you can believe that." Bo smiled. "But I have help. Jeanne, my wife, she runs the restaurant and tries to keep food in him, which isn't easy these days. Elise, she works here with us. She checks in on him. Keeps him riled up, not that it takes much. He's presently ticked at her 'cause she's gotten sober, and he's running out of folks to get drunk with."

Bryce scoffed. "Hell, if that's all it takes… We'll get along fine."

They climbed the steps which led onto the deck that ran along the side and around back of the restaurant. Gerald McNabb was nowhere in sight.

"Lost him already?" Bo said, snickering. "Fifteen minutes into your first day?"

Bryce arched his brow and pointed toward the front door.

"Yeah, he eats inside, always the same booth. Always the same order. He'll sit there two hours and might take more trips to the head than bites of his food."

"Well," Bryce said, checking his watch, "I got plenty of time."

Bo turned and glanced toward the marina, where several boats were slowly approaching the fuel dock. He said, "I better get down there. New hire gets flustered pretty easy," then gave a wink.

"Okay," Bryce said. "Wish me luck."

Bobby Tolliver heard the faint rumble of a car engine. He dropped the socket wrench into a rusty metal toolbox and wiped his hand on the leg of his Dickies coveralls. He came out of his garage and walked to the edge of the bluff of his hillside property. Standing there with his long, skinny arms hanging at his sides, he peered down into the inhospitable valley above which he'd spent the sum of his thirty-three years. He could make out headlights on the paved, serpentine road that bisected the valley before degenerating into a narrow, precarious dirt road that climbed the eastern slope of Mount Jenkins. He checked his watch in the moonlight: 11:52 p.m.

He heard ringing and returned to the garage, where an avocado-green rotary phone sat atop a workbench. He lifted the handset to his ear.

"We got company comin'," his cousin Danny said.

"I seen. What kind of company, you reckon?"

"At midnight? The uninvited kind." Danny Tolliver blew out a breath.

"The Chevy," Bobby said through clenched teeth. "It's the owner of that Chevy Apache. I *told* Terry—"

"Easy, coz," Danny said, sounding worried but composed. "I couldn't reach Terry. Becky said he got called in, but he didn't answer at the sheriff's office."

"So, it's on us," Bobby said grudgingly.

"Listen, this guy comes up our hill, he's illegally trespassin' on our family property," Danny said, indignant. "We got every right to turn his ass around 'fore he gets to the shed. And if he don't wanna...we'll teach the motherfucker a lesson."

"What're you thinkin'?"

"Maybe some early fireworks?" Danny suggested.

Bobby instinctively glanced at Miss June 1969 gracing the pinup calendar his boss had given out as a Christmas gift. "All right." He exhaled. "Shit."

"I'll meet you at the turnaround," Danny said.

Bobby slammed the handset into its cradle, grabbed a book of matches, and dropped it in his pocket. He ran around to the side of the garage and found the galvanized fuel can in the tall weeds, set it on the seat between his legs, kickstarted the little Kawasaki 250, and tore through his property and into the dark woods, headlight off, traversing the trail by memory and instinct.

Bobby reached the embankment that sloped down to the only spot along the narrow road wide enough for a vehicle to maneuver a turnaround. He cut the engine and coasted down to where dozens of tires lay stacked in a dry-rotted heap amongst the trees.

He fishtailed to a stop and laid the bike in the underbrush. Glancing over the hill, he saw Danny struggling to drag a fallen tree across the road just ahead of the turnaround. In the distance, he could see the vehicle's headlights moving up the mountain. Bobby scampered down the embankment to help his cousin.

After rendering the road impassable, they took cover up on the hill behind the wall of rubber. Danny worked a tire free and held it upright while Bobby poured kerosene into its cavity.

A long, two-toned utility vehicle came around the blind bend and skidded to a halt, its long hood buried in the bushy blockade. A man wearing a tan safari jacket and dark slacks cautiously stepped out of the vehicle. He inspected the obstruction, tugged half-heartedly on one of its branches, and walked back to the open driver's side door. With his hands on his hips, he began to survey his surroundings.

Through small gaps, the Tolliver cousins watched the man's gaze settle over the cluster of tires concealing them. The man stared for a long moment in their direction, then turned and leaned inside the vehicle.

"Goddamnit." Bobby lit a match.

The tire gained speed as it barreled toward its intended target, eventually smacking against the back door, and ricocheting into the air. Flames showered down on the vehicle's white roof and its operator's back.

They quickly prepared a second tire. Bobby held a match over the puddled kerosene. It ignited immediately. He heard a crackling sound and felt a stinging pain. *"Fuck."* He pounded the back of his hand against his chest to extinguish the burning hairs. Then, incensed, Bobby whispered, *"Hit* him this time." Danny launched it down the slope.

Just as the driver spun around and aimed a long barrel in their vicinity, the blazing BFGoodrich slammed squarely into his midsection with a sickening thud.

Bobby watched the man's arms thrash wildly at the flames dancing from his jacket. He eventually shed it from his body, and through the dark smoke, Bobby could see him sling it to the ground. He took a few quick steps away and brought a hand to the right side of his head.

When the Suburban's back door began to open, Danny said, "Time to book," and disappeared back into the woods on foot.

Bobby grabbed the fuel and struggled back to his bike, slipping on dead leaves and walnuts. He raced along the trail ducking branches, squeezing the can between his thighs.

Pulling into his yard, the porchlight shone on his fifteen-year-old daughter, BJ. Then came Loretta bounding toward him, letting out her humanlike yelps. He cut the engine and coasted to the side of the garage, allowing Loretta a chance to identify him along the way. He parked the bike and returned the fuel can to its place in the weeds.

Bobby was shaking and damp with sweat as he stepped onto the porch. "BJ." He took a moment to catch his breath. "Whatcha doin' up, girl?"

"Loretta heard your motorbike take off and started barkin'," she said, glancing at the dog who was squatting in one of the sparse patches of grass. "It scared Tucker. Where did you—"

"Go on, now, get ta bed," Bobby said, then spun around and scanned the valley. With his back still turned, he repeated tersely, "Go on, I said. Get in there and let Tucker know everything's okay, and y'all get back to sleep." Then softly, "Love ya."

"Love you too, Daddy." He heard the screen door open, and BJ say, "C'mon, Loretta. Let's go night-night, girl. C'mon, go night-night?"

Bobby stood on the porch until he spotted taillights moving steadily down the mountain. He went into the garage and called Danny. "They're headin' out."

"We...'bout..." Danny stammered, out of breath but excited. "'Bout...got our heads blowed off."

"Let's go clean up. I'll swing by."

Bobby grabbed a small fire extinguisher from under the workbench, a flashlight from a cubbyhole, and the ring of keys hanging from a nail. He headed back up the mountain in his pickup truck.

When they arrived, the two tires were smoldering, filling the air with the thick, pungent odor of kerosene and burning rubber. Bobby extinguished several flaming puddles, and Danny kicked dirt over the evidence. Together they cleared the road of the tree.

"Let's give it a check," Bobby said, nodding further up the mountain. They got back in the truck and headed to the shed.

It was an old, corrugated metal building, camouflaged naturally by decades of overgrowth, and artificially by assorted hues of green and brown spray paint. Bobby worked the lock and pulled open one of the sliding doors by its handle. Danny pointed the flashlight inside, immediately illuminating the jacked-up skeleton of a '61 Chevrolet Apache pickup truck, their most recent acquisition.

As a mechanic at a gas station auto repair shop in the nearby town of Olivia, Bobby was tasked with tagging any worthy prospect that came in for service, then skimming paperwork for the owner's address. They'd choose a night when his big brother was on duty. With Deputy Terry Tolliver patrolling the immediate area in his Sheriff's Department Plymouth cruiser, one of their crew would attempt to gain entry by peeling the rubber seal from the driver's side window and working a homemade metal tool with a carefully formed hook on the door lock mechanism. Then hotwire the thing. If successful, it would be driven to the southeast corner of Myer County to a shed located on Tolliver family property high atop Mount Jenkins. There, it would be carefully dismantled and sold off in pieces and parts through various channels Terry had established.

If the door couldn't be compromised or their electric finagling failed to turn over the engine, the next morning its owner would likely discover cinder blocks in place of its wheels, thus ensuring their efforts weren't for naught.

The men stood inside the shed, Danny probing its cavernous interior with the flashlight. The place smelled of grease, mildew, and stale cigarette and pot smoke. Detecting nothing out of order, they turned to leave.

As Bobby pulled the handle, he thought he heard a faint sound distinct from that of the screeching door. He paused in the early morning silence. It came again. This time, both men heard the female voice. "Help."

They squeezed through the opening, and Danny searched again with the flashlight.

"Please. Help me?"

They followed the voice to the far corner of the building. A young girl sat on the oil-stained concrete floor behind a massive rolling tool chest. In the glare of the artificial light, she appeared to be roughly the age of BJ. Maybe older. She was nicely dressed in a short red floral print dress with a white collar and big white buttons down the front. Her long, straight hair was neatly parted in the middle; two hair clips held her bangs away from a face baring a mixed expression of hope and terror. She wore white patent sandals, her exposed toes painted bright red. Around one of her ankles hung a thick, padlocked dog chain, similar to one which had recently gone missing from Danny's property. It was secured to the rusted rear axle of a 1960 Ford F-350.

CHAPTER

4

INSIDE THE RUSTY Anchor, Bryce spotted McNabb sitting alone in a corner booth, his back to the small dining room. He went over and slid onto the opposite bench.

A pretty waitress wearing a straw cowboy hat and a light-blue Rusty Anchor tank top came up and glanced at Bryce. "Coffee?" She turned over the thick white mug in front of McNabb and began filling it from a black-and-gold pitcher.

"Yes. Please," Bryce replied.

She filled Bryce's mug with steaming coffee and set the pitcher on the table. "I'll leave that with you. Know what ya want, Nabby?" she asked, winking at Bryce.

"Number one," McNabb said.

"How do you want your eggs?"

"Runny." He glanced at the menu. "Bacon. Crisp."

"Grits, hash browns, or breakfast pota—?"

"Hash browns." He thrust the menu toward her.

"Toast or biscuits and—"

"*Toast,*" he snapped. "Dry."

She smiled, showing dimples and kind eyes. She snatched the menu from McNabb's hand and looked at Bryce. "And for you?"

"Same," Bryce said. "Right down the line."

"I'll get those orders put in." She turned and walked away.

Bryce's eyes followed her, moving from her cutoff jean shorts to her calves to the back of her white high-top Converse.

McNabb took a few sips of coffee, removed the reading glasses from his breast pocket, and positioned them atop his red, bulbous nose. He opened the magazine he'd brought and began scanning it purposefully.

"Nabby?" Bryce said.

"Not to you, fella," McNabb replied from behind his magazine.

Bryce nodded amenably. "So...they said you eat breakfast here every day?"

"Sometimes lunch. And sometimes supper," he replied. "'Cept on Mondays when they close up. Mondays I stay aboard *Betsy* and eat my snacks and drink my beer. *Alone.*"

Bryce said, "Okay. I'm a beer drinker too."

Apparently unimpressed by the revelation of their shared interest, McNabb turned a page and continued reading, his mouth parted slightly.

Bryce shook his head, then fiddled with his cell phone until their food arrived.

"Two of everything," the waitress announced and began setting down plates.

They ate in silence. Bryce could hear his own stomach groan as the greasy food made its way through his compromised digestive system. There was a moment when he wasn't sure it was ready for sustenance, but eventually there seemed to be a reconciliation among the elements. By the time he finished sopping up the last puddle of egg yolk, he was certain he'd be able to match the previous night's intake later that evening at the tavern.

Bryce wiped his mouth and glanced at McNabb. The poor man had cut his food into tiny pieces and, with his fork trembling, was mindlessly pushing things around on his plate, never taking his eyes off the folded magazine held in his free hand. Then, without a word, McNabb set down his fork and magazine, scooted out of the booth, and headed for the men's room.

Bryce freshened his own coffee, then refilled McNabb's nearly empty mug. When he returned and noticed his cup had been filled, McNabb gave Bryce a bloodshot glance, then returned to reading and playing with his food.

In the silence, Bryce skimmed the printed items neatly arranged under a piece of Plexiglas that covered the top of the table. They were of the vintage sort, yellowed advertisements for regional businesses and attractions cut from newspapers, brand ads including Virginia Slims and Royal Crown Cola, and a few promotional flyers and dog-eared brochures for the nearby resort town of Partonsburg. When he'd covered those, he killed a good ten minutes trying to identify the quasi celebrities in the framed eight-by-ten glossies on the wall. All of them had, it seemed, eaten at the Rusty Anchor, and taken the time to thank its owners with a scrawled personal message.

Bryce nodded at the wall and said to McNabb, "You got any portraits of yourself? You could sign one and be on the wall of fame up there."

Gerald McNabb glanced at the wall, then at Bryce, then back at his magazine.

Resigned to McNabb's impenetrable obstinance, Bryce logged into an online betting site to check the odds on that night's fight.

A group of older folks climbed noisily into the booth directly behind McNabb, jarring his bench seat in their effort. McNabb scowled. Once settled, they began chatting. Bryce noticed one male voice dominating the conversation, talking loudly over the others. Apparently, it was a continuation of an ongoing conversation.

"So...Metamucil's the answer," a woman said, followed by a round of laughter.

Then the loud man crowed, "Now normally, I'm as regular as the mail. I eat, then I crap."

A different woman began, "Mama used to give my daddy boiled prunes and—"

The loud man interrupted, "And when I'm done, I'm up and out. I don't linger."

The woman made another attempt. "Mama used to take her Harlequins in with her and—"

"I can't sit there that long," the loud man butted in again. "I gotta get off that thing. My legs start goin' numb from the diabetes. When I had that constipation spell last month, my bowels locked up tighter than Dick's hatband. I sat there so long, when I's done, had to wiggle my toes and roll my ankles around, get the circulation going 'fore I could stand. Till Sally here got me on that Metamucil."

McNabb put down his magazine, slid out of the booth, and stepped up to theirs. There were four of them, a couple per side. The pair on the opposite side stared uneasily at McNabb while the man babbled on, oblivious.

Eventually, the loudmouth, sitting on the outside with his back to McNabb, followed the gaze of his boothmates to where McNabb hovered over his shoulder. From what little he could see, Bryce figured the man to be in his late sixties or seventies. He was red-faced and overweight, the table's edge pressed deep into his big, round belly. He looked up at McNabb, spittle in the corner of his plump, purplish lips. He cleared his throat and asked, "How can we help you, sir?"

"You think anyone wants to hear 'bout how steady you shit?" McNabb began. "How the hell can I eat my breakfast…"

The pretty waitress hurried over and asked the party of four, "What can I get y'all to drink?" and began handing out menus.

Bryce grinned.

As McNabb made his way back to his seat, the obnoxious man said, "Hey, speakin' of appetite killers, how 'bout you buttonin' up?"

There were stifled snickers. Bryce suppressed a smile as he watched an indignant Gerald McNabb climb into the booth, his bare breasts jiggling.

No sooner than he'd settled back into the booth, McNabb grabbed his magazine and scooted out of it, purposely bucking against the back of his bench in the process.

Bryce looked up from his phone.

McNabb said, "I'm done," and shuffled away.

Bryce took a quick sip of coffee and went to the register to pay their bill. He gave the waitress money from the petty cash he'd been provided, then glanced out the window as she rang him up. McNabb was halfway back to his boat.

"He seems especially pleasant today," she said, nodding at the window.

"Yeah, I don't think he cares much for me."

"Well, that puts you right in there with pretty much…the rest of us. 'Cept Marta. He likes her. Used to like me, but I stopped drinkin' with him."

"Oh. You're Bo's niece?" Bryce asked.

"Yep. Elise," she said, handing him the change.

"Well, Elise. Have faith, I *will* break through. Just need a little more time. I haven't really turned on the charm."

She laughed and said, "Oh, I see. Yes, crank that charm of yours up to eleven, and let's see where it gets ya."

"I will, and you *will* see. I got"—he glanced at the Corona Light wall clock—"over six hours left with dear Mr. McNabb. Or *Nabby*, was it?"

Elise grinned and asked, "How many *days* you got with him?" and gave a wink.

"Through Tuesday, Miss Smarty. Minus Monday. Marta's back Wednesday." Bryce arched his brow. "Not convinced, are you? Care to wager? Say...twenty bucks?"

"Twenty bucks on what?" Elise asked gamely.

"Nothing crazy, just...by breakfast Tuesday morning, Mr. Gerald McNabb, renowned grouchy old bastard, and yours truly"—Bryce crossed his fingers—"are thick as thieves."

"I'll take that bet. Breakfast. Tuesday. If I spot *any* sign of a budding bromance, a Jackson you shall have." Elise held out a hand and they shook.

• • •

As soon as Bryce's foot touched the deck, he heard, "You ask permission to come aboard another's vessel, fella."

Bryce's face warmed with embarrassment as he backed his way up the gunwale steps and onto the dock. He couldn't see McNabb but assumed he was lurking behind the dark screen of the enclosed cockpit. "Permission to come aboard?"

"C'mon," McNabb said, with a trace of contrition in his frog-like voice.

"Sorry 'bout that," Bryce said. "Must be an old tradition. My dad has a boat, but he's never made anyone—"

"Might just be common goddamned courtesy," McNabb shot back. "Take a seat. Clock's tickin.'"

Bryce checked his watch.

When Gerald McNabb emerged, he held two cans of Natural Light in the crook of his arm. He handed one to Bryce, then popped the tab on the other.

"Uh...I'm pretty sure I'm not supposed to consume alcohol while—"

McNabb snorted.

"And I just had a three-plate breakfast and three cups of coffee," Bryce said.

"Well, reckon it'll be my next," McNabb said. He grabbed the unopened can from Bryce and set it on the small table between them. "Sit."

They both sat, and for the next few minutes, not a word was spoken. Every so often, a boat would glide past them heading out for a day on the water. Bryce returned waves and pleasantries; McNabb ignored them all.

The old man emptied the first can and reached for the second. He opened it, took a long pull, sank further down in the chair, and splayed his legs. Bryce grinned at his little hairless legs and knobby knees.

The second beer disappeared as quickly as the first. McNabb went into the cockpit and, after a considerable commotion, emerged with a small Coleman cooler. He set it at the foot of his chair, then pulled a beer can from the pocket of his shorts.

Bryce rubbed his stomach and said, "Think I've got some room in there now, if you don't mind?"

McNabb pointed at the cooler.

"Thanks." Bryce reached down, dug out a cold can, and shook off the ice and water.

Again, they sat in silence, drinking their beers. Bryce's

ringtone went off. He reached into his front pocket, checked the screen, then replaced it.

McNabb grunted.

Finally, Bryce said, "Nice view from here," while scanning the layered mountain ranges in the distance.

"Mm."

"I hear you quit takin' her out. *Betsy*."

"Didn't *quit*. I *stopped*. Hell of a difference."

"Does she run?" Bryce asked, then drained the last of his beer.

McNabb ignored the question and nodded toward the cooler.

"Thanks."

"Me too," McNabb said, crushing an empty can in his hand and dropping it onto the deck.

Bryce opened two fresh cans and handed one to McNabb. As they steadily consumed their beer, *Betsy* began to rock. McNabb slammed his can down on the table and struggled to his feet. Facing portside toward the marina, he threw his arms in the air and screamed, "Slow down, damnit!"

Bryce peeked around the old man and spotted the object of his wrath: a fancy sport boat turning into the fuel dock, bringing some good-sized rollers in its wake.

McNabb took advantage of being on his feet to duck into the cockpit. He returned with a fresh six-pack of Natural Light, pulled each can loose from the plastic rings, then shoved four of them into the ice. He set two on the table and fell back into his chair.

Bryce got one, popped it open, took a drink, and settled his gaze on the mountains again. "I've lived here in the foothills my whole life, but I don't go up into the mountains much anymore," he said sincerely. "They've mostly just been...*there*. Like a backdrop, you know?"

"That so?"

"My sixth-grade class spent a week at a little camping community up in the park. That was cool. Guess it's more fun when you're a kid."

McNabb scoffed, causing Bryce to glance over at him.

"We did the whole campfire thing every night. I remember this one teacher, Mr. Kidd, would tell us stories. Try to scare us. Something about how the Indians believed there were evil, child-eating creatures that hid in the mist, you know, down in the valleys. That's about all I remember, so I guess the story sucked."

"*Sha-con-a-ge,*" McNabb said, pronouncing each syllable deliberately.

"What's that?"

"*Where's* that," McNabb corrected. He nodded toward the mountains. "That's what the Cherokees called 'em. The place of blue smoke."

"Oh, okay," Bryce said, followed by another long silence, which McNabb seemed quite comfortable with.

Triggered by a memory, Bryce said, "We had to take showers together, the kids. Well, the boys...you know. It was kind of weird for most of us at first. There was just a long wall lined with shower heads and no, like...privacy. That first night, we all took off our towels real shy like and walked around with our hands covering ourselves. But by the end of the week, we were running around laughing and trying to smack each other's butts as hard as we could. Then we'd all vote on who had the reddest handprint on their—"

"Good for you," McNabb said disconcertingly, then

turned his head portside and stared out at the cove. "That's how it should be for youngsters, right? Fun and games."

Suddenly uneasy, Bryce fell silent again.

McNabb took a pull from his beer and said, "What if I told you there *were* evil creatures in them mountains and that they did indeed prey on children?" He crushed the empty can in his hand and tossed it behind his chair.

Bryce snickered. "I would bet you'd tell me the same story Mr. Kidd told us that night by the fire."

"Shhht. You'd lose that bet, fella," McNabb said.

Another long silence followed.

After a while, Bryce glanced over at McNabb to find him sleeping peacefully in his chair. He pulled out his phone and texted Katie, "He's passed out," followed by a laughing emoji. "Guess I'll be home sooner than I thought."

IT HAD BEEN well over an hour since they discovered the girl in the shed. Bobby pulled the Jeep pickup into his gravel driveway. He went straight to the garage and came out with a tight grip on the neck of a fifth of Old Crow. He kept it hidden as if his late wife were still there to disapprove.

After a long, throat-burning swig, he screwed on the lid, then pulled a pack of Camel cigarettes from his pocket and tapped one out. When the phone rang, he went back into the garage and lifted the handset. "Yeah."

"What the *fuck* did you do?" Terry Tolliver asked his little brother.

Bobby hesitated. Then said lamely, "What?"

"The tires. What the hell were you—"

"Savin' our asses. That dude with the Apache's on to us. I told you he was back at the shop that next mornin' talkin' to my boss. I'm thinkin' he seen—"

"Well, there's the problem," Terry said. "You was thinkin.'"

"D-don't do that," Bobby said hurtfully. "Danny said let's try and stop him at the turnaround. So he don't get to the shed."

"Oh? Danny said? When, exactly, did dipshit Danny start givin' orders to anybody?"

"We was tryin' to—"

"Shut. Up. Bobby," Terry said in a whispered growl. "That

man, the one you lit up?" Terry exhaled. "He was with a very important gentleman...come down from Ohio."

"Wha—Ohio?"

"Hold on," Terry said. Bobby could hear a muted discussion. When Terry came back on the line, he said, "Okay, listen, brother. My dumb-as-fuck baby brother..."

There was a long, tense silence. Bobby could hear his own heart pulsing in his ears. Finally, Terry said, "I guess this's on me, now. But you understand somethin'..."

"What?" Bobby whispered.

"You don't take orders from nobody but me. Ya hear? Startin' right now, you listen only to me."

"Yeah. Okay."

Terry sighed. "I gotta book."

When the dial tone sounded, Bobby replaced the handset. He ran fingers through his long brown hair, took another swig of whiskey, then wiped his wet, bushy mustache with a forearm. After returning the bottle to its hiding place, he lowered the garage door and went inside the house.

In his bedroom, Bobby glanced at the unmade bed as if expecting April to be there sleeping soundly. He peeled off his shirt and stood in the middle of the room, letting the cold air from the window unit blow over him. Soon the small room reeked of the acrid odor of his armpits. He went to a bedside table and removed the imitation-pearl-handled Bauer .25 ACP that Terry had gifted him a few months earlier. Deputy Tolliver had accepted the pistol from a half-awake, red-eyed kid he pulled over late one night. The high schooler was more than eager to exchange the little pistol in lieu of an escort to the drunk tank.

Back outside, Bobby sat on the porch with the gun in

his lap, struggling to decipher the events of the previous few hours. He smoked a cigarette. Then another.

Bryce was climbing *Betsy's* starboard steps, eager to get home, when he heard McNabb say, "My grandparents spent their whole lives there, up on Whistle Mountain. And I spent my summers there. Then, after my daddy died..."

Bryce stopped midway up the steps and turned to him. "Thought you'd left me there for a second." He checked the time on his phone's screen and descended back onto *Betsy's* aft deck.

McNabb made a long sound like a wild hog, leaned over the port gunwale and spat. Then he continued with his story as if no time had elapsed. "My daddy would take me and Mama up there to my grandparents' log home. Mama called it the homeplace. These were her folks. Daddy never wanted nothin' to do with them mountains and was sure as hell not gonna spend weeks on end up there with us. My Grammy would say he's 'cityfied.' So, he'd drive us up there every summer, drop us off, and go back home and probably nearly drown himself without Mama there to moderate his drinkin.'"

Bryce returned to his chair and covertly texted Katie an update.

"Then, one summer, Daddy didn't show up to get us. It was 'bout time for school to start back home, and we were still up there with no word from Daddy. Mama got real worried. It...took a good while to get news up there, so damned isolated. I remember bein' in the garden with Grammy pickin' veggies for dinner. Mama was sittin' on the porch snappin' beans. Just as the sun was goin' down, up the dirt drive came this tall, white off-road-type vehicle with big tires, like you got on your truck. Looked like a Jeep but said 'Toyota' on the grill."

"A Land Cruiser," Bryce said, settling in again. "They can look like Wranglers. My friend's dad has one, sixty-eight model. He spent almost thirty thousand dollars restor—"

"In this *Land* Cruiser was a man and a woman, both dressed in fancy clothes, least seemed to me. Both wearin' dark sunglasses. The woman took hers off, got out, and stood by the vehicle with her hands clasped in front of her short skirt. She had an expression of pity as she eyed each of us. The man jumped out, came around and stopped in the middle of the yard. He wore these crazy striped pants and boots with a big buckle on the side. Tall fella. He wanted to know if a Zoe McNabb, that's Mama, lived there. He was wavin' a piece of paper in his hand. He had news for her..."

McNabb patted his shirt pocket, pulled out his reading glasses, and set them on the little table. He dug further, coming up with a small cigar and lighter. He lit the cigar and took several quick puffs, then blew a stream of smoke into the air and said matter-of-factly, "The man read from that piece of paper he was holdin'. What it said was that Daddy had been killed in a car wreck comin' back from Alabama. He and a bunch of buddies had met up for their little...reunification. He left late one night headin' home, stopped for gas, and somehow or other got back on the interstate goin' the wrong way."

"Oh..." Bryce said, startled by McNabb's blunt summation.

McNabb shook his head and was quiet for a moment. "Only thing I remember after that was thinkin' how it didn't seem right that these fancy-lookin' folks in this big shiny machine could be deliverin' such goddamned awful news."

"Who..." Bryce caught himself. "I'm sorry about your dad."

"Eh. He wasn't much of one, truth be told. But it was still a...*shock*."

"You were how old?"

"Maybe nine. Ten."

Bryce's phone vibrated and chimed in his pocket. He ignored it.

McNabb eyed Bryce's pocket. "Girl?"

Bryce nodded.

McNabb waited a beat, then continued. "Grammy had been listening to the whole thing. She came out of the garden, went straight to the woman standing by that truck, and handed over the basket filled with fresh-picked vegetables. As thanks for coming all that way."

"That was cool," Bryce said sincerely.

"Well, it's all she had to offer."

Bryce nodded.

"So, *who*, you were about to ask, were these alluring bearers of shit news?" McNabb savored his cigar a moment as Bryce fidgeted. "Say, what's your field gonna be? You just doin' this for fast summer cash...or you goin' into healthcare of some sort?"

"Premed," Bryce said. "Doing this will be good for..." He stopped and scratched his neck. "It's good experience...in the field."

"Mm-hmm," McNabb said. He took a few puffs, exhaled smoke, then picked a piece of tobacco off his bottom lip.

"Think you can hold off *Toots* long enough to listen to a dyin' man for a bit?" He patted his own pocket, referencing Bryce's phone.

"Sure," Bryce said. "That's part of—" He stopped himself before completing the condescending statement.

McNabb scoffed. "Well, whatever your reason for bein' here, like we used to say on the playground, 'Tag, you're it.'"

Bryce let out a nervous laugh. Despite the youthful reference, he sensed some gravity in the old man's tone.

McNabb nodded again toward the rolling peaks of the Southern Appalachians. "Well, turns out, the couple in the Jeep, the Land Cruiser, were members of some fancy resort on the other side of the mountain. Someone who worked there had received a call, wrote down the information, and this couple volunteered to make the trip over to deliver it.

"After reading the note, the man put it in his pocket and got back in the driver's seat. Mama was kinda moanin', then she started wailin', 'No. No. No!' The woman went up on the porch and knelt beside her.

"After a while, Mama calmed down. I was just pacin' the yard, kickin' dirt around, not knowin' what else to do. The woman came down off the porch. She was real friendly. Said she was sorry about my father. She glanced up at my mama on the porch, then back at the man in that Toyota contraption. She gave me a sympathetic smile. Even at my young age, I could tell she really felt for us...for our loss."

Bryce's forehead wrinkled. "There was a resort on the other side of—"

"It was there," McNabb said with finality. "The whole time. Grammy just didn't want me to know about it."

"Why not?"

"She was a mountain woman. She didn't trust rich folk.

Thought they was highfalutin, cityfied, like Daddy." McNabb scoffed. "See, its founders, back before the park and its almighty decrees, they created the whole thing as a huntin' lodge...and fishin'. But when they opened the park, what had been a modest sporting retreat became a summer playground for their rich and spoiled descendants...second- and third-generation members. They even built a big hotel up on the hill above all the old huntin' cabins. Then some of 'em started building their own nice, new cabins. Grammy would say these next generations were a bunch of ingrates. Living off their folks' hard work.

"My papaw had an old .22 caliber bolt action rifle he used to hunt game with. One day the park rangers showed up and let him know there'd been complaints of gunfire. Grammy and Papaw knew sure well who's complainin.'"

McNabb popped open a beer and took a long drink. "Here's the thing...my Grammy knew everything that went on 'round that mountain. There was a grapevine 'tween a few of the old women. I remember Daddy tellin' me 'bout a friend of Grammy's who'd been reported to the rangers for settin' traps near the resort. No one was hurt, but some of them kids stayin' there came up on one while they was out explorin.' Told their parents.

"Now, the resort relied on this one local dairy farmer to provide them with milk during the busy summer months. Well, after they report the old woman, next time that dairy farmer goes out and sets a bucket under ol' Bessie, he squeezes out blood."

"Whaaat?" Bryce said, more amused than amazed.

"Grammy was a healer; this old gal was somethin' else altogether."

"Somethin' else?"

"Daddy didn't believe in that folk magic hocus-pocus. But I think he liked seein' my face when he told me them stories. Anyway, I remember one night, Grammy and Mama sittin' out on the porch and me runnin' around catchin' lightnin' bugs. I had a mason jar; I'd stabbed holes in the lid. That thing was plumb full. When I went up on the porch to show Grammy my spoils, I thought I heard her say somethin' about them 'hurtin' girls over there.' When I asked, 'Who's hurtin' girls?' Grammy told me it was grown-up talk and to get back out there and catch me some more bugs."

"But she gave them those vegetables," Bryce said.

"She did. It was important for Grammy to be...respectful. So she thanked this man and woman for their deed, even though she didn't care for them, probably feared 'em."

"You ever find out what she meant about hurting girls?" Bryce asked.

"Not from Grammy. And she died just a few years after Daddy."

"Sorry. And your poor mom," Bryce said sincerely. "Lost her husband and mother that close together. How'd your grandmother die?"

"Stubbornness. One mornin' she was choppin' wood. Like she done a million times. The axe hit funny, never sunk in. It come back on her shin. Wasn't even that bad a cut. At first. She didn't believe in real medicine. Didn't trust no doctors. Back then, least up there, they used plants for all kinds of 'cures.' Passed down from their ancestors. And the Indians. She concocted a paste, salve, made from the bloodroot plant that grew on the side of the mountain along the river. Grammy'd pick them every fall. It's got a big, pretty white bloom. But it's the root that's used. She applied that paste to her cut. She told Mama she knew it was workin' 'cause of how bad it hurt when she rubbed it in. Thought that meant it was *drawin' out* the impurities. Didn't do nothin' but burn the skin right off her leg down to the bone. Mama and her got into these bad shoutin' fights. Mama wanted her to see a doctor, but Grammy wouldn't have it. By the time Mama finally got her to a doctor outside Partonsburg, Grammy was crazy with fever...and hallucinatin'. She'd made herself a necklace. Stuffed pieces of bloodroot stem into a black walnut...a charm to ward off uninvited spirits. She wouldn't let go of that damned charm. Didn't work, though. The spirit of death came and took her, invited or not. Infection had spread too far."

"Superstition—" Bryce began.

"Well, these days folks know most of the so-called healing properties of the plant are utter horseshit. But they still sell it in some of them kooky *nature* stores. Indians, they thought it cured all kind of ills. So Grammy made tea from it, said it soothed her sore back, eased her headaches, said she couldn't get to sleep without her bloodroot tea at night. She said it like 'rut'...bloodrut. She would dye her baskets and clothes with it too. Her fingers were stained with the juice that came off the roots. Reddish-orange gunk. That's where it got the name."

The ringtone went off on Bryce's phone.

"Ah... Toots again," McNabb said. "Well, don't keep her waitin'. Answer the damn thing."

Bryce stood and pulled the phone from his pocket. "Hey, what's up?" He made his way astern for privacy. The old man snorted behind him, and Bryce glanced back to catch him shaking his head and scratching his chest, his fingers buried in the shaggy patch of gray hair between his sagging breasts.

"How's it going?" Katie asked.

"Well, it started off suckin' ass," Bryce whispered. "I tried talkin' to the guy…like, usin' some of the *starters* they suggested for me, you know. But I was gettin' like…fuckin' crickets. Didn't say jack to me the whole breakfast."

"Oh no. Uh…why do you sound drunk?"

"Well, I'm aboard *his* vessel. And…when aboard someone else's…you…obey the captain's orders."

"Okay, Gilligan. A better question: Why are you always blaming others when you overdrink?"

Bryce changed the subject. "So, we're on for tonight?"

"We're on," Katie confirmed. "Paaartay! I called Erin and reserved the private room. There'll be eight or ten of us."

"Okay, we'll—"

"Hey, my boss just came back here," Katie whispered. "Better run."

"All right. Go. Bye."

He walked back to his chair. Sitting atop the little table were two fresh beers and a pint of blended whiskey, the label of which he didn't recognize. Bryce said, "You tryin' to kill me or somethin'?"

"A woman wants a man who can hold his liquor. Need to exercise your liver if you wanna impress Toots."

"I must have impressed the hell out of her last night."

"Ah. Last night, huh? Well, then"—McNabb raised the little bottle—"hair of the dog, fella." He took a swig and handed it to Bryce, who was shaking his head.

"I appreciate the offer, but I got a long night ahead of me."

• • •

They were lounging in the bow of Bryce's father's Chaparral with a beer cooler at their feet.

"He finally started telling me about the time he spent

on...uh...Whistle Mountain, I think?" Bryce said to Katie and Garrett. "When he was a kid."

"*The* Whistle Mountain?" Garrett said with interest. "Why haven't you heard of it? I mean, like, some shit went *down* in that place. I'm tryin' to remember..."

"Well, I'm sure I'll hear more tomorrow."

"Ooh, good," Katie said. "Bring me back a juicy story."

"Apparently there's a big resort there—"

"Was," Garrett chimed in. "They leveled the whole deal, what was left of it. Not too long ago."

"Were you ever up there?" Bryce asked.

"Yeah. My dad and I used to hike all around there. You could take a trail right up to it."

"Shoot," Katie said, giving Bryce's hand a squeeze. "That would've been cool to hike to."

"Too late, Toots," Bryce said.

"Nah, uh-uh," Garrett said, laughing. "You did not just call her *Toots*."

WHEN BOBBY CAME into the living room the next morning, BJ was lying on the couch with her head on the armrest. At the opposite end, seven-year-old Tucker sat cross-legged, a plastic bowl of cereal balanced on his lap, watching cartoons on the big Zenith television. Loretta, stretched out below them on the dingy shag carpet, let out a low growl as Bobby approached. "Hush it," he said.

Loretta owed her life to little Tucker and BJ. Danny, one of the many Tolliver kin populating the insular community of Mount Jenkins, along with a family friend, had met the Staffordshire bull terrier while unwittingly attempting to steal the very vehicle under which she slept. The little dog had shot out from the cover of the Bronco in a brindle blur and executed a quick and ferocious attack. The two stunned men hustled off beyond the reach of the dog's lead. They stood, hands on knees, catching their breath as the dog barked incessantly, her short muscle-rippled hind legs kicking grass and dirt into the air.

On the drive back to Mount Jenkins, each man cursed profusely, examining his body, tallying puncture wounds.

She'd done her job well, and for the next two nights, the little nuisance would enjoy her routine of sleeping undisturbed under the high clearance of her owner's 4×4. But Danny, forever seeking bait for his fighting bullies, returned with reinforcements a few nights later. It took all three grown men, in multilayered clothing, to wrestle her into a cage in the back of the El Camino. Danny cataloged two additional wounds for his collection.

When BJ and Tucker came across the dog at their cousin Danny's house the next day, the befuddled dog instantly bonded with the children, and a reluctant Danny relinquished her to his young second cousins.

Bobby examined the blue morsels scattered within his son's bowl. "Yer gonna poop green again."

"Good!" Tucker said.

BJ stuck her bare foot under his nose. Tucker jerked his head away, a look of disgust fixed on his face. His bowl tilted just enough to spill milk on his leg. "Daddy!"

Bobby grinned and pointed a finger at BJ.

On the grainy screen, Bugs Bunny popped his head out of a hole, snapped off the end of a carrot, chewed, and scanned his new surroundings.

Bobby left for the kitchen to make coffee.

• • •

At half past noon, Bobby was sitting on the tailgate of his beat-up Jeep Gladiator lunching on a Whopper and fries when he heard the service bell ring. He glanced over at the gas pumps and saw his brother's motorcycle. Terry Tolliver slowly threw a leg over the seat of his '67 Harley-Davidson Electra Glide. He stood tall and muscular, having retained the build of the once feared all-state defensive end. He grabbed his belt and pulled up his blue jeans, then adjusted his mirrored sunglasses. As the attendant approached, Terry unlocked the gas tank lid, then spun the keys on his finger.

"Regular?" the teenager asked.

"Yeah." Terry did a 360-degree check, then swaggered toward Bobby, the wood soles of his weathered cowboy boots clicking on the asphalt. He called back, "Don't you spill none, neither."

"Yes sir," the kid yelled.

Terry stood towering over his little brother for a moment, neither man speaking. Finally, he put a boot up on the tailgate between Bobby's splayed legs, removed his sunglasses, and rested a forearm on his thigh. "Workin' hard?"

"Takin' my hour lunch break like everyone else," Bobby said, not looking up from his burger.

"So..." Terry said.

Bobby took a big bite, chewed, and wiped mayonnaise off his mustache with a napkin. When he lifted his drink and began sucking on the straw, Terry smacked the nearly full cup out of Bobby's hand, splashing ice and soda into his face and sending the cup tumbling across the parking lot.

"So..." Terry repeated. "Found some bolt cutters, did ya? Hero?"

Bobby's jaw tightened as he considered his next words. "Why was that girl chained—"

"Our friends in Ohio..."

"I don't got no friends in Ohio," Bobby said, drying his face with a sleeve.

"But Daddy did. And at the time he and Mama tried to drive up that oak tree, apparently Daddy owed 'em one. A big one. So, they're here checkin' on some of their investments in the area. They asked me to line up a few interviews. That girl, she was interested in a...hostess position at one of their establishments. So, they needed to...check her credentials, you might say."

"You kiddin' me, man?" Bobby said.

"Don't get all righteous on me, little brother. Like you ain't went to a few poon shacks back in the day. 'Fore April, rest in peace." Terry shook his head. "I've always protected you, but...they get any idea you tried to kill—"

"I wasn't tryin' to kill nobody. I didn't know..." Bobby lowered his head. "I told you, I figured it was the owner of that Chevy tru—"

"*Then* they lose a potentially highly profitable asset."

"Asset?" Bobby said. "That wasn't no *asset* chained up in that shed, like one of Danny's damned dogs. Looked more like a terrified girl."

Terry's big hand clamped Bobby's jaw. "Hey," he snapped. "Shut up and *listen* up." He jerked Bobby's face upward. "And *look* up, dummy."

"What are you into?" Bobby managed to ask through his twisted mouth.

"I ain't *into* this. This ain't my scene. You get me?"

He let go of his brother's face. Bobby worked his jaw around.

"Anyway, it's an easy fix..." Terry slid his boot off the tailgate and eased on his sunglasses. "Where's the girl?"

Bobby stared at the ground and shrugged his shoulders. "Gone."

"Gone where?"

"Don't know. I dropped her off at the strip mall outside Olivia. Then I come straight back home."

"That right? Well...s'pose she's gone all right." And with that, Terry took a deep breath, turned, and walked wide-shouldered and bowlegged back to his bike. Bobby heard a loud squeal as the big motorcycle peeled away from the station. He looked over to see the young attendant standing by the pump, startled, still awaiting payment for the fuel.

•••

That evening, Bobby left the gas station garage just before six o'clock and drove downtown to the Smoky Cove Tavern. Bear Brownlee, the owner's son, had recently returned to his hometown after serving his country in South Vietnam. He'd promptly taken charge of the family business. Bear had always been cordial, despite Bobby's hippy-like appearance. Bobby ordered three meals to go, and Bear poured him a draft while he waited.

Behind the bar hung a corkboard covered with an assortment of items: pictures of staff and patrons, business cards, and notices for upcoming live music. A white piece of paper caught Bobby's eye, the word "MISSING" in large block letters across its top. The photo underneath was of a young woman: age seventeen, hair blonde, eyes blue, last seen wearing patchwork blue jeans and a white baseball shirt with yellow sleeves, the word "Partonsburg" in red letters across its front. It was not the girl from the shed.

He arrived to pick up BJ and Tucker at Danny's house just as the sun was disappearing behind the hills to the west. At home, they ate fried chicken dinners on TV trays in the living room. Bobby and BJ took the couch; Tucker and Loretta spread out on the floor. After back-to-back episodes of *The Twilight Zone*—Tucker's choice—Bobby sent them off to brush their teeth. Later, in the kids' shared bedroom, Bobby sat on the edge of Tucker's bed and, per routine, asked about their day.

"Loretta got in a fight with Lulu," Tucker said excitedly. The dog was curled up in the crook of the boy's legs.

"Who's Lulu?" Bobby asked.

"One of the bitches Danny has locked in the pen behind their house," BJ promptly explained.

Tucker's eyes got big. Bobby gave her a look.

"What?" BJ shrugged her shoulders. "That's what they're called. Bitches. It's in the encyclopedia."

"Yeah. And yer havin' way too much fun sayin' that word." Bobby noticed Tucker's animated expression and smiled, then slapped his leg playfully.

"Ow!" Tucker said and began laughing and kicking at his dad. Loretta grumbled but didn't move.

"Why won't Danny let them come inside his house, like he does Loretta when we're there?" BJ asked.

"Those he keeps in that pen, he breeds them with other dogs to make puppies."

"To fight?" BJ asked. "Like the ones on those big chains. The ones we aren't allowed to pet."

"Hey, let's not worry about what Cousin Danny does at his own house. That's his business, right? He gave y'all Loretta, didn't he?"

"Yeah," Tucker asserted. "He gave us Loretta."

"Was he gonna make Loretta have babies too?" BJ asked.

"Uh...yeah. But then she took to you two clowns, and Danny loves y'all. So..." He looked at Tucker and changed the subject. "That show we watch spook ya?"

"Nah, I don't get scared no more. Loretta'll protect us."

"Yeah," BJ interjected. "She barks at every little noise outside and attacks the window."

"Good," Bobby said. "I don't have to worry about you. Loretta's on guard."

"That's right," Tucker said, nodding. "Anyone try to break in our house, she'll do what she done to Lulu."

"What she *did* to Lulu," BJ corrected.

"I know she will," Bobby confirmed. "Now...everyone. Get. To. *Sleep*."

Bobby went to the door and glanced back at them. "Night. Love ya. See you in the morning."

"Night. Love ya. See you in the morning," they returned in unison.

He switched off the light and closed the door.

"Hey," Bobby heard his daughter whisper.

"What," Tucker whispered back.

"Loretta's a bitch."

"Wha...Daddy!"

"Shhh!"

CHAPTER

8

Sunday morning Bryce and Gerald McNabb sat for breakfast at the same time at the same booth and ordered the same food as the day before. The only difference being a noticeable easiness between the two, which Elise seemed to pick up on. At one point, McNabb even freshened Bryce's coffee. Elise offered an approving nod from behind the register.

Back aboard *Betsy*, the two returned to their plastic chairs, and McNabb immediately lit a cigar.

"You feelin' okay today?" Bryce asked.

"Like a million bucks. You?"

"Maybe like...a hundred," Bryce said. "I was enjoying hearing about Whistle Mountain. Well...unfortunately, your grandmother...passing away..."

McNabb shot him a questioning glance.

"And something about the resort on the other side..."

McNabb pulled a white handkerchief from the back pocket of his shorts and cleared both nostrils. After eyeing the results, he folded it twice, leaned to his side, and returned it to its place.

Bryce wondered why he'd watched the entire act rather than look away.

"Yeah," McNabb said. "I loved my Grammy. Mama sent me over to that resort to get help so we could bury Grammy

119

next to Papaw in the cemetery. Up in them woods behind the house. That same couple from before, in the big white Toyota, and another man drove me back to the homeplace. I was in one of the back seats that face inward. Never seen that before. They helped us dig a grave for Grammy right beside Papaw's. We didn't have no fancy marker like the one Grammy had made for him—had all kinds of symbols etched into it that I didn't know what were. I remember askin' Mama. All she said was that they's nonsense and to stay away from the cemetery. Said, 'It ain't no place for children.'

"When we were done, that kind woman from the resort made us all hold hands and said a prayer. While she was prayin', I peeked and seen the two men grinnin' at each other. That man with the boots with the buckle, he caught *me* catching *them* and gave me a little wink."

"What an asshole," Bryce said.

"Well, I doubt he knew Jesus from a jellybean. 'Heathens,' Grammy called 'em. When that lady from the resort said that my Grammy had went to a better place, even I wondered how the hell it's better to be rottin' in the ground than livin' and breathin' above it." McNabb scoffed. "Daddy didn't let us go to church.

"The man I'd never seen headed back to the truck. Me and Mama stood there with the couple for a while. Mama was cryin' and had her hands on my shoulders. She kept pullin' me closer to her. I just remember wantin' to run. Just run as deep into them woods as I could go. But I knew Mama needed me there with her.

"The woman looked around at what I'm sure to her was outright squalor. Then she said, 'I think they could find some work for you over at the resort.' I saw her man shoot her a look, but she ignored him. She knelt down and said, 'It gets pretty busy around Independence Day, that's when our summer season gets going. It's almost here. You look like a big strong boy. Think you could carry suitcases up the hill to the hotel for folks? The money could help y'all out. Help your mama.'

"Then the man yelled from the truck, 'Stuart, let's move it, man,' and they left.

"I figured Mama wouldn't want me anywhere near there after all Grammy had said about the place and its people. Turns out, she *made* me go. Guess she was worried 'bout us not havin' no money and wasn't sure how else we's gonna make any.

"See, my grandparents adapted. When the park came, Papaw couldn't hunt no more with his guns, so he took to trappin'. They grew their garden, and there was the little river nearby that Papaw fished. They'd also become honey farmers. Papaw had beehives. They'd go tradin' over at a few of the markets in them little mountain towns, haulin' jars of honey, fresh produce, and Grammy's handwoven baskets to trade. Sometimes they'd go as far as Partonsburg when they was real low on cash. But Mama? She didn't know how to take care of herself. She'd never had to. I tried to keep up the garden after Grammy died. And I fished the river. But Mama? I think she kinda checked out on me.

"So, off I go to the big, wicked resort, where they apparently *hurt* people, to hustle baggage up and down them goddamned steps fifty times a day.

"There was folks runnin' every which way over there. Stuart was the one I answered to, mostly. He's the man who drove the white Land Cruiser. He was my boss. He was always real mean to the others. Reckon he was halfway decent to me on account of his wife's sympathetic nature. But I sensed he did *not* care for me one bit. And there was this weird little man, name of Gaspar. I knew him best. He was goofy and made me laugh. He carried a walkie-talkie radio hidden under those long, crazy shirts he wore. There'd be someone saying somethin' you couldn't really understand 'cause of all the static. Gaspar'd yank his shirt up, grab the radio and go, 'Ten-four. I'll take care of it, sir!' Then he'd look at me and say somethin' like, 'My boss says you been stealin' bread from the kitchen. Ordered me to strip you down and cover you in syrup and tie you to a tree and let the bears eat you.' It was always somethin' different, always silly. But this once, when he pulled up his shirt, I seen a gun under there. So I reckon Gaspar wasn't all jokester.

"What they did," McNabb said, gesturing with his hands, "was they hauled guests from a parking lot further down the mountain in this big green-and-white Suburban. Gaspar was one of the drivers. Soon as I seen him pull that thing up at the foot of those stone steps, I'd run to the back of it and start unloading while Gaspar helped everyone out. He'd always say something nice, like 'Please enjoy your stay and let us know if there's anything you need.' Blah, blah, blah. Or, if he knew them well, he'd joke. 'Mr. Latham, good to see you again! Don't forget, no sex with the wildlife. Remember last summer?' Ha, ha, ha. Reckon he was more goofy than funny.

"Then I'd start haulin' the luggage to the hotel way up on the hill. There was about forty of them steps, and steep, especially for a fella like me, twelve years old and built like a fireplug. Short little legs. I'd usually get a quarter per trip. Maybe two or three from some of the bigwigs. Good money come the end of the day for a young'un, and this was 1969.

"When Thursday came around, the day before Independence Day, that place got as busy as one of Papaw's hive boxes.

The whole day I was up and down them steps and doin' whatever else they asked me to do. I remember I was walkin' around back of the hotel collecting trash. There was this one strange room that was always dark inside. I wasn't allowed to go into the room, I'd just knock on the back door, and this man would open it, and I'd wait there. He wore those western-type shirts, cowboy shirt. He would pull the plastic garbage bag from under the bar and spin it closed, then tie the end. I always thought that was cool and he knew it. He'd wink when he handed it to me.

"I carried the bag across the parking lot behind the hotel and threw it in the dumpster there at the edge of the woods. When I turned around, one of them long green-and-white Suburbans pulled into the parking lot. The driver got out. This man, he's got something white covering the side of his face. He walks around the vehicle and opens the back door. Reaches in and just pulls this girl by both arms. She wasn't puttin' up no fight; she could barely stand. But I'm tellin' ya, fella"—McNabb arched his brow and pointed his finger at Bryce's face—"that girl, and she was just a *girl*, she looked me straight in the eye, and the expression on her face...I won't never forget.

"I hid around the side of the dumpster and watched him and that girl go across that gravel lot, her still in her pajamas, barefoot, and disappear into them woods behind the hotel."

"Oh sh-shit," Bryce said.

"Yup." McNabb produced a small whiskey bottle, took a long pull, then handed it to Bryce. "Here ya go, fella."

Bryce drank, then handed it back to McNabb, who took another drink. The bottle was passed back and forth as the implication of the disclosure pervaded the heavy silence.

"So, your Grammy was…uh…right about the p-place," Bryce finally mumbled.

McNabb studied the kid's boozy eyes. "Hell, I best get to the nut of this 'fore *you* check out on *me*."

Bryce returned a silly smile. "Nah, I'm good."

McNabb snorted. "When Gaspar sent me home that evening, I started walking my usual way, past the newer cabins, the ones down in front of the hotel. When I come out the other side of the woods, I seen Mama with Stuart. They was standin' near the far end of the big tree that'd been made a bridge over the river. He was talkin' and shakin' his head a lot. Mama wasn't movin'; she just stood there lookin' down, listenin'. He pointed back toward the resort. That's when he saw me crossin' over. He put both hands on her shoulders and said somethin', turned, and started comin' my way. His face…he looked pissed. As we got near each other, 'bout midway on the bridge, I started movin' to the side, you know, to go around him, but he blocked my way. I tell you, fella"—McNabb tapped his chest—"my heart was a thumpin'. I wouldn't look him in the eye; I just looked down at the water pourin' over them big rocks. Then he moved right in front of me, kinda blocked my view of Mama. He wrapped his big hand around the back of my neck and squeezed. Not like he was hurtin' me, but he had a pretty good grip. He said somethin' like, 'Awful good of your mama to let you come here and work. Sounds like you're makin' out pretty well.' Reckon he could hear me jinglin', every pocket of my overalls was filled with coins. He tightened his grip and pulled me closer. 'Don't you go givin' your mama any trouble, now. You hear me?' I twisted out of his hold, and boy I beat feet across that bridge.

"On the way back to the homeplace, I asked Mama why

she was over there near the resort. She told me she just wanted to see it for herself, and that was all she said about it.

"That night, we ate corn and sliced tomatoes from the garden and buttered homemade sweet bread Mama got from an old lady who came around tradin' once a week.

"Mama put me to bed early that night with a cup of tea. Said Grammy had left a bunch of herbs in the back room. She'd found some bloodroot and made me tea like Grammy done. Said it'd help me get a good night's sleep, since the next day was July Fourth and it'd be a long workday. She made sure I drank every drop of that tea before she tucked me in for the night. It didn't taste nothin' like Grammy's.

"I remember Mama closin' my door and me just layin' there in the dark. Then I remember wakin' up to these poppin' sounds outside. Not right outside, kinda distant. I sat up in my bed, and in my mind, I kept seein' that girl's face. That one bein' drug into them woods. How scared she was. Kept hearin' Grammy sayin' them girls was bein' hurt over there. Then I seen a vision of that girl standin' right by my bed, like a ghost... Her hand reachin' out to me, that expression on her face."

McNabb's own face tightened, and he turned away. He took a few deep breaths and gazed out at the calm waters of the cove. He removed a small knife from the pocket of his shorts and carved off the tips of his fingernails. Then, he lit a cigar with a few quick puffs and spat a piece of tobacco out of his mouth.

"What I'm 'bout to tell you, this ain't nothin' I'm proud of..." He turned back to Bryce, only to find him slumped over in his little plastic chair, eyes closed, breathing steadily.

"Well, touché, you punk son of a bitch."

• • •

When Bryce peeled open his eyes, the sky was bloodred across the horizon, transitioning into oranges and yellows, and finally a dark purplish blue. The setting sun's reflection drew a straight orange line on the water's surface across the main channel, through the little cove, past the fuel dock and marina, and touched *Betsy*'s portside.

Bryce sat alone on her aft deck in the little plastic chair. There was a sharp pain behind one eye, and when he sat up, his vision blurred. He let out a deep hiccup that brought with it the burn of alcohol-infused bile. "*Fuck.*" He got to his feet slowly, fighting for balance. He took a few steps and clung to the flybridge ladder until his surroundings ceased spinning. Another violent heave sent fluids up his throat. He stumbled to the starboard gunwale and spat into the water.

Once the threat of vomiting had passed, he straightened and called out, "Mr. McNabb?" Squinting into the screened enclosure, he saw no movement and heard no reply. He shook his head at the crushed cans of Natural Light littering the deck, the empty whiskey bottle overturned on the table. Then he climbed out of the boat and meandered down the dock toward the gate, his phone vibrating in his pocket.

CHAPTER

9

ON WEDNESDAY OF the following week, July 2, Bobby was inspecting the carburetor on a '66 Mercury Park Lane when his boss stepped into his bay and signaled a phone call.

Bobby quickly cleaned his hands with GOJO, then went into the office and took the handset off the desk. "This is Bobby."

"Bobby, they took Terry to Foothills Trauma Center." It was Danny. "He wrecked his bike late last night. Sounds like he busted his leg real good, but that's all I know. I'm on my way there."

Bobby hung up without another word and left work.

He rushed through the facility's front entrance and into the waiting room. Danny was sitting in a chair against the wall. Bobby sat down heavily beside him. "Any word?"

"Nothin' much. Just been here a few minutes. Becky's back there with him."

Bobby ran a hand through his long hair. "Where'd it happen? The fuck was he doin' out ridin' around late at night?"

"Don't know and don't know," Danny said, shaking his head. "Got a smoke? I left without…"

"Yeah," Bobby said, then scanned the crowded room. He nodded toward the doors.

127

They smoked outside in front of the large window, keeping an eye out for Becky.

After a few minutes, she spotted them through the window and marched outside, flustered, her eyes red and tired.

"What they sayin'?" Danny asked.

Bobby lit a cigarette and handed it to her. She took a deep drag. "His leg...it's plumb busted all to pieces," she said, her voice catching. "They had to make it straight again with some kind of splint to...hold it together. It's swollen up real bad. They say they gotta do surgery later...put screws..." Becky began to sob, smoke billowing from her nose and mouth.

The men shared a concerned look. Bobby put a hand on his sister-in-law's shoulder. Becky closed her eyes and took a few forced breaths.

"They let us see him?" Bobby asked.

"Yeah. Not for long, though. He's in one-eleven."

"Go on, Bobby," Danny said. "I'll stay with Becky."

"They got him on morphine," Becky warned. "So he's all...spacey."

Bobby eased the door open to room 111 and stuck his head in.

A big smile spread across his brother's face. "There he is," Terry said weakly.

"You alive?" Bobby joked, gauging his brother's temperament.

"I am. Think my leg died, though," he said, his smile fading.

"What the hell happened, man?" Bobby asked.

"Ah...I laid her down," Terry said, his smile now gone. "Gonna be okay. Just outta commission a while."

"What can I do? You need me to get your bike home? Where's it at?"

"Nah, taken care of." He winced, and a single tear ran from the corner of his eye.

"You hurtin'? Let me get someone."

Bobby stepped out into the hallway and waved down a nurse. Soon she was in the room fiddling with the bag above Terry's head. "So you're feelin' a lot of pain?" she asked.

"It's kickin' pretty damn hard," Terry informed her.

"I've upped your dose. Should start easing." On her way to the door, she said to Bobby, "Might wanna wrap it up soon, hon. That medicine'll make him wanna sleep."

"Right on," Terry said, his system already enjoying the boost of the narcotic.

The nurse giggled and winked at Bobby as she backed out the door.

Bobby walked around the bed and sat in the recliner by the window. He was silent a moment, watching his tough older brother breathe, his arms crossed over his chest, rising and falling steadily. He noticed no other marks on Terry. No road rash, no abrasions on his knuckles or elbows, not a scratch on his face.

"Just your leg, brother? You didn't—"

Terry shook his head, his lower lip quivering. "Just the leg." Then his face contorted.

"You'll be okay," Bobby whispered as he stood. "I'll let ya rest." He patted his brother's hand and left.

In the waiting room, Bobby found Danny and Becky sitting together sipping coffee from small paper cups. Danny met him in the middle of the room. "Can I see him?"

"He's out," Bobby lied. "Give him a little bit."

Danny nodded. They walked back to Becky and sat on either side of her. Bobby asked, "Anyone from the sheriff's office come by?"

"Uh-uh. Not a one of 'em."

Bobby thought for a moment. "Who brought him in?"

"Lord. I...I don't know. My mind was goin' ever which direction." She looked toward the ceiling and closed her eyes. "I'm sure they told me; I just wasn't hearin'."

"Do you need anything from your house? Reckon you'll be here a while?"

"Yeah, I'll stay the night. They ain't gonna move him till he's more stable, so...I'll need...just enough for the night...my meds, toothbrush, toothpaste. And there's a book on my nightstand..."

Bobby walked around to the back deck of Becky and Terry's house where the key was hidden under a potted plant. Inside, he went down the hallway and into the master bath, where he found three amber bottles on the sink where Becky said they'd be. He gathered the other items she requested and threw them all in a small duffle bag he'd taken off a closet shelf. In the kitchen, he set the bag by the back door, then went to a narrow side door that opened into a small storage garage. Terry's Harley-Davidson rested on its kickstand along the near wall. His helmet hung from the tasseled handlebars. Both the machine and helmet were unblemished.

• • •

Bobby was back at the hospital by 6:00 p.m. Danny and Becky were both in the waiting room.

"Anything?" Bobby asked.

"Nah. They ran us out," Danny said. "He was in a lot of pain, and they've got him on a heavy drip."

Bobby set the bag at Becky's feet. "Should be everything."

"Thank you, hon." She stood and hugged him. "Yuns go home to your families. I'm fine."

"I'd like to see Terry before I leave," Bobby said.

Becky nodded. "If they'll let ya."

Bobby waited until the receptionist spun around in her chair to open a file drawer, then snuck past her. He peeked in room 111, checking for staff. It was empty but for the patient.

He stood over his brother, watching Terry's eyes roll around lazily, a dumb smile on his face.

"Gotcha on a hefty dose, I hear," Bobby said.

"Man...I ain't feelin' nothin' but...goooood," Terry sang, then let out a slow laugh through clenched teeth.

"Glad to hear it," Bobby said. "What happened to your leg? Wasn't no motorcycle wreck. You can bullshit the staff, but Becky'll know...she ever goes in that garage."

Terry's expression turned to one of mock surprise. "Aaah. Little brother...figured it aaaall out, man."

"What do I got figured out, Terry? Tell..." Bobby stopped speaking; his mouth remained open. He ran a hand through his hair and began pacing the room. Finally, he said, "That Ohio bunch done this to you? Over that girl in the shed?"

"You been watchin' too much *Ironside* or somethin', man." Terry let out a low, hoarse laugh.

"I'm sorry, Terry," Bobby said, his face twisting in grief. "Oh, man. I'm so fuckin' sorry."

"It's aaall cool. Aaall copacetic." Terry's head sank deeper into the pillow. "Go on home," he said, just before drifting off into a morphine slumber.

• • •

When Bobby pulled up to Danny and Deidra's to get the kids,

he found BJ uncharacteristically quiet, and Tucker exhausted and despondent. Loretta had gone missing at some point during the day, and Deidra had taken the kids out to search the hills and valley for nearly two hours on her and Danny's Honda CTs. With darkness falling, they reluctantly returned to the house without the dog.

The mood was somber as they ate Salisbury steak TV dinners in the living room that night. So devastated were the kids about Loretta, it wasn't until they were tucked into bed that either thought to ask about their Uncle Terry.

"He'll be okay," Bobby told them. "But his leg is hurt pretty bad, and he's in a lot of pain."

"Deidra said he crashed his motorbike," BJ said.

"Yeah, but he's okay. Just take a while to get it healed up so he can walk on it."

Tucker asked, "Will he be in a wheelchair?"

"Oh, I don't know about that. Maybe crutches for a while." Growing impatient, Bobby said, "Hey, we'll find Loretta."

"Sissy was shootin' bottle rockets off the back porch. All the dogs was howlin'. I bet Loretta got scared and ran away," Tucker offered. "We went all over callin' for her."

"She probably didn't come when we called 'cause of the stupid name you gave her," BJ told her little brother. "She already had a name. Didn't they tell Cousin Danny her name when he adopted her?"

"M-maybe Danny wanted y'all to give her a new name. Somethin' special."

"Yeah." Tucker looked at his sister defiantly. "And *you* said Mama's favorite singer was Loretta Lynn and that her daddy was a coal miner like Loretta's."

"She was," Bobby confirmed. "Your Papaw Whitaker was a coal miner in Kentucky too. Harlan County."

BJ scoffed. "That dog looks like she's been diggin' around in...a c-coal mine," she said, her voice breaking.

"Well..." Bobby wondered if her rare show of emotion was due to the missing dog or talk of their mother, who BJ was old enough to remember. "Her name is Loretta now, and we're going to find her, so don't worry."

He kissed Tucker on the head, then went to BJ. He reached down to wipe her wet cheek, but she turned away and did it herself with the palm of her hand.

Tucker sat up. "Sissy, can I sleep with you tonight?"

"No."

Bobby frowned and said, "We'll find her tomorrow, Tuck." Then he kissed the back of his daughter's head and whispered, "'Fore you fall asleep, you tell your mama you love her. She hears ya."

•••

The next morning was July third. Bobby woke before sunrise. He made coffee, took a mugful to the front porch, and lit a cigarette. With all the previous day's drama, he realized he'd not checked the mail. He went to the plastic mailbox at the end of the long driveway, removed its contents, and closed the lid. Walking back, he noticed the open window to the kids' bedroom, the screen laying on the ground below it. He darted back toward the house, taking the porch steps in a single leap, then slung open the screen door and ran through the hallway and into their room.

Tucker shot up in bed when his daddy burst in. Bobby went to BJ's bed and threw back the covers. He shuddered as if struck by a blast of cold air.

Tucker rubbed his eyes and glanced at the empty bed. "Where's Sissy?"

"Go make you some cereal, Tuck," Bobby said, shielding his son from his discovery. "Go on."

The boy did as he was told.

With Tucker gone, Bobby reached down and removed Loretta's collar from his daughter's pillow. He held it up and studied the brownish stains, then crammed it into his pocket.

CHAPTER
10

T HE MAN CALLING himself Winston Wakefield paused at the top of the long stone staircase. He caught his breath while taking in his surroundings. The hotel itself, which lacked any identifying signage, was a long two-story wood-framed structure painted white with a deep porch that spanned its length. Folks were scattered about, leaning on the porch railing, or sitting in rocking chairs, relaxing and chatting, cocktails in hand. Delighted children scurried around the grounds holding sparklers over their heads, letting out high-pitched squeals. He flinched at the loud, whistling swoosh of a firework that soared into the night sky behind the hotel and exploded in a series of short glittering bursts. Cursing under his breath, he started toward the hotel's entrance, forcing smiles at those he passed on the way.

In the first-floor lobby, a massive stone fireplace stood as the room's nucleus. On either side, vast gathering spaces held distressed leather sofas, an assortment of chairs and small tables, with area rugs scattered about. The walls displayed old, framed photographs of groups of people, hides of sundry woodland creatures, as well as an enormous two-man logging saw and other tools and gadgets from a bygone era.

Making his way to the reception desk situated in the far-right corner, he passed game tables, clusters of sitting areas, and a candle-lit dining room behind glass-paned double doors.

He fell in line behind another man who was speaking in hushed tones to the male receptionist. After a short exchange, the guest disappeared down a dark hallway. The man stepped up to the desk and nodded to the smiling receptionist, who asked kindly, "Hello, sir. May I have your name?"

"Winston Wakefield."

The receptionist peered down, referencing something outside the man's field of vision. "Okay," he said, then gestured in the direction the previous guest had departed. "Follow the hallway to its end. The gentlemen's lounge will be on your left. See the bartender; he'll take care of you from there, Mr. Wakefield."

"Thank you," he replied, then hesitated, expecting to be given a key. "I had reserved a cabin for—"

"Yes, sir. Head straight down the hallway, the last door on your left. They'll assist you from there. Enjoy your...time, Mr. Wakefield."

The hallway was dimly lit by wall sconces spaced between framed sepia photographs documenting the region's early century logging boom. He heard a noise ahead of him and slowed as a shadowy figure emerged at the end of the hall. A man held open a door and waited. He wore a tweed bucket hat pulled low on his head and white bandages covered one side of his face.

The man calling himself Winston Wakefield quickened his pace and said, "Thank you," as he passed through the doorway. He paused just inside the smoky room.

The bandaged man came up beside him and said, "See the bartender." He pointed toward the far end of the narrow room where a tall, slender man wearing a black-and-white snap-button western shirt and a scarlet ascot was working the bar. His black hair hung long, and lifeless, dark sideburns crept down his sunken cheeks. He leaned on his elbows and began speaking to a guest standing at the bar.

"The bartender, Roy Rogers over there," the bandaged man repeated, "he'll take care of you." He then turned and left the lounge through the same door they'd entered.

The room was much like the interior of seedy beer taverns the man had frequented in his wilder years, before the wife and the kids and the seventy-hour workweeks. Its walls were paneled in dark wood, the ceiling covered with stamped tiles. Several tall round tables lined the middle of the room without chairs or stools. And there were certainly no girls parading about. There were no females whatsoever, only men, standing alone, sipping drinks, their heads hung low.

He went to the bar as instructed and waited to be acknowledged. The conversation beside him ended with a short burst of laughter, and the cowboy bartender swaggered over to him. "Need a drink, man?"

"No, thank you," the man answered with mounting unease.

The bartender tapped a thick turquoise ring twice on the lacquered bar top. "Nah, you'll have a beer," he said, examining his customer with pale, dead-looking eyes.

The man stammered, "Okay, yeah. Just...anything's fine."

The bartender filled a glass from the tap and swiped the foam head with the handle of a pair of steel ice tongs. He wiped the tongs on a hand towel hanging from his shoulder, then took a cardboard coaster from atop a tall stack and skimmed it across the bar. He set the glass on the coaster in front of the man.

"Thank you."

The bartender's hand disappeared and reemerged holding a white card with black print. He placed it on the bar and said, "Mark your selection."

The man glanced at it, perplexed.

"It's required," the bartender explained, handing the man a yellow pencil. Then, he licked his lips and said, "Mmm-mmm. Good selection tonight."

The man silently scanned the card.

"First time?" the bartender said. He retrieved a pack of cigarettes from under the bar and tapped one free. "It's cool. Add a zero to the dollar amount. You'll pay me, cash, right here. I'll thank you for your patronage, you'll leave me a generous tip, and you'll be escorted to your cabin. When you're done, you will not return to the hotel." He lit the cigarette and took a long drag, turned his head, and blew smoke through the side of his mouth. "Someone will pick you up at your cabin and take you back to your vehicle."

The man read through the list. A drop of sweat fell from his brow as he mindlessly checked the box beside "1954 Pinot Gris."

"Oh, yeah. Fifty-four...*good* year," the bartender said, then clicked his tongue and winked.

"What? What's so good about it?"

"Only aged fifteen years," he explained. "Gonna have that fresh, *savory* bouquet." He pulled a black waiter wallet from his back pocket and set it on top of the bar. "Put the amount inside," he ordered, then took the pencil and wrote *5* at the top after the printed word "Cabin."

The man calling himself Winston Wakefield mechanically counted out the bills while the bartender talked on a radio he'd retrieved from under the bar. Soon Gaspar, the little gimpy man, appeared at the back door.

The man placed the wallet beside his nearly full glass of beer and walked hesitantly toward the exit. *Fifteen?* he thought, a wave of shame washing over him.

139

CHAPTER

11

Bobby didn't know why he drove to the hospital without calling 911. One minute he was telling his son to make a bowl of cereal, the next he'd come through the kitchen and practically dragged him to the truck. On his way up the mountain to Danny and Deidra's, his mind raced. By the time he pulled up to their house, he was nearly hysterical.

"Unchain them dogs, let 'em run loose in the pen," he told Danny as he paced their yard frantically. Then he handed him the little Bauer semi-automatic. "Keep this on you. BJ's missin.'"

When Deidra came out onto the porch, Bobby told her BJ had stayed the night with a friend. Danny shot him a look but did not dispute the claim. Bobby apologized for the early hour. "I gotta get somewhere quick and don't know how long I'll be gone."

At Foothills Trauma Center, he tore through the waiting room and into the long hallway without checking in at the desk. In room 111, Becky sat reclined but awake under a beige hospital blanket in the chair by the window.

"I need to talk to my brother," Bobby said.

"What's wrong?"

"Please, Becky."

She stood, squeezed her husband's hand, then ambled to

141

the door. She stopped and asked Bobby, "Do you want some coffee?"

"No."

As soon as the door clanked shut, Bobby said, "Someone took BJ." Simply uttering the words caused him to break down. "She's g-gone, Terry." He began to sob uncontrollably.

Terry grimaced, then took a labored breath but said nothing.

"You'll get her back for me." It was not a question. "You..."

Terry lay motionless and silent.

Bobby studied his brother for a moment. As he walked around the bed toward the recliner, he noticed Terry avoiding eye contact. He sat on the edge of the chair's cushion, elbows on his knees, and examined his older brother lying there on the hospital bed: the big, handsome face, the elevated leg in some sort of contraption, the strong, tanned hands. A wave of nausea rippled through him, and he fought to keep from retching.

"You...you know who else is missin'?" he managed to say.

Terry didn't respond.

Bobby kicked the metal frame of the bed, causing Terry to wince and reach for his battered leg. "The dog. Our dog's missin'. The dog that would've never let this happen. The dog that would've fought to her death to protect them kids."

When Terry showed no reaction, Bobby turned away and stared out the window. Then said distantly, "I'd've taken a bullet for you. For Becky."

At this, Terry raised himself onto his elbows. "I've always been there to protect you—"

"Fuck, *protect* me. You *did* this to me. T-to my little girl."

"She ain't *yours*," Terry said, gaining fervor. "You forget? She just come with the package."

Bobby said slowly, "I ain't never treated that girl but she weren't my very own. Same as Tuck."

Terry scoffed. "Well, ain't you a special cut. Get outta my sight."

"I ain't in your sight," Bobby grumbled. "'Cause you're too sorry to look me in the eye."

Terry shook his head slowly, then let his lids fall over his pink-rimmed eyes.

"Terry," Bobby snapped. He grabbed his brother's arm. It was as heavy and lifeless as a piece of firewood. When Terry began to snore, Bobby cursed and walked out.

Upon his return to the waiting room, he saw a Myer County Sheriff's deputy, whom he'd met once or twice through his brother, standing over Becky, speaking quietly. Bobby lit a cigarette and joined them.

The deputy gave him a nod. "Bobby. Real sorry, man."

Bobby returned the nod but said nothing, knowing well enough not to trust his brother's fellow lawmen. He'd grown up on stories about federal revenuers clashing with bootleggers, prostitutes working out of trailers parked behind restaurants and bars, and citizens of note having repeated DUIs dismissed. All the while Sheriff Nathan Tolliver and his obedient subordinates stuffed wads of bills into their pockets. Bobby had no doubt that his big brother, like their father before, was firmly entrenched in the good ol' boy network.

Bobby stared at the deputy's face, then turned to blow smoke into the air. He nodded again at the deputy and said to Becky, "I'll check back."

• • •

Later that night, with Tucker sleeping over at Danny and

Deidra's, Bobby sat on a little stool in his garage drinking from his bottle of Old Crow. Side one of the Stones' *Beggars Banquet* played on a cheap phonograph he kept on his work bench. The phone rang. He answered, "What?"

"Bobby?"

"Yeah." He didn't immediately recognize the distressed voice. *"What?"*

"Terry's dead."

"Becky?"

For a moment, he listened to her erratic breathing. Finally, she said, "He got a hold of the sleeping pills in my purse. Took 'em all. Mixed with the morphine in his system..." Becky lost her voice.

Bobby's whisky-soaked mind attempted to process the revelation. Memories came in chronological order: running onto the football field after a high school game, a scrawny little sixth grader getting knocked around while searching for his big brother's number fifty-four jersey. Then Terry's graduation from the academy and the pride of standing beside his big brother in full uniform. Seeing Terry's picture alongside their father's in the local paper under the headline containing the word "Inquiry." Terry standing beside him as an endless line of people filed past hugging and shaking hands and telling them how sorry they were as their parents lay in polished boxes, their faces pale and unsmiling. The gratification he felt when Terry recruited him into the family's illicit enterprise after Bobby was hired on at the station in Olivia.

Next, he pondered that drunken night at Danny and Deidra's home. Everyone was out back around the bonfire, drinking and smoking and moving to the music of the famous crooning brothers who'd begun their careers performing on local television and radio programs. Bobby had stepped outside with an armload of fresh beers and caught Terry with his hand on April's waist. He watched his older brother slide his hand slowly toward her breast before April slapped it down and moved away from him.

He remembered Terry's complete absence following April's unexpected death, her heart having stopped days after giving birth to their healthy baby boy. The undetected condition too arduous for Bobby to pronounce.

Finally, he fought to recall Terry ever having demonstrated the faintest interest in his only niece. For Danny, a loving relationship had seemed natural and effortless, he and Deidra always there for him with unconditional support at a moment's notice. Same with Becky. Not so for her Uncle Terry. No, he'd never cared about her, much less loved her.

Bobby took a long pull from the bottle.

"Bobby? You there?" Becky whispered.

He took a deep breath and let it out, nodding his head slowly. "Yeah."

"Terry left a note," Becky said in a small voice. "Says it's...for you."

"Yeah?" Bobby replied listlessly.

CHAPTER
12

GASPAR GRINNED AND nodded at Winston Wakefield, the man he'd only recently chauffeured to the resort. He did a silly dance move and sang out, "Oh yeah. My man's ready to groooove."

"Stop it," the man said curtly.

Gaspar seemed hurt, and said, "Peace, brother," as the man brushed past him.

The U-shaped rear of the hotel contained a graveled parking area filled with vehicles of a more modest variety. Gaspar led the man onto a narrow, wooded path which sloped down to a wider, perpendicular dirt road. There was the sound of water flowing close by. Gaspar went left and continued down the road, spinning a ring of keys on his finger. The man followed.

Tiny, rustic cabins appeared nestled in the trees on the right side of the road. Moonlight shimmered in the riverbed beyond. In stark contrast to the hotel proper and the newer, refined cottages which fronted it, cabin five, like its counterparts along the unlit dirt road, was a primitive wooden structure with a dilapidated covered porch. The rusted metal roof sagged under the weight of years of accumulated debris. It appeared utterly deserted but for the yellow glow in its front windows.

The man had been faithful thus far in his eighteen-year

marriage, never remotely approaching infidelity. Yet here he was, seizing the opportunity, consciously fighting to keep his mind singularly focused on that which awaited him. His heart convulsed wildly against his sternum, a symptom of carnal anticipation for a lascivious encounter like those he'd heard about at his colleagues' recent happy hour rendezvous. Or, perhaps, the result of cardio-wrenching contrition.

"So," Gaspar said, "there's an ice cooler in the little kitchen in back...stocked with beer. Sweet thing'll be in the bedroom waiting." He made a popping sound with his mouth. "When you're done, you put out the lamp in the front room by, you know"—he mimicked twisting a knob—"turn the round thingy till the flame goes out. Then you sit there in the front room, *alone*, and I'll swing by and..."

Fifteen. The age of his only daughter.

The man rushed up the porch steps, opened the front door, stepped inside, and closed the door behind him. He was met promptly with a heavy, musty odor and a noticeable rise in temperature. Outside he heard footsteps on the porch, then the dead bolt clicked. He went to the window, pulled back the curtain, and watched the little guy's limping silhouette heading back in the direction from which they'd come.

A stone fireplace sat dormant in the far-right corner with cheap furniture fronting it. Near the window by the front door, a simple wooden chair sat beside a small table which held a tarnished-brass oil lantern, its flickering flame giving the room its only light.

The man walked directly into a dark, narrow hallway which ended at a closed door. He placed both palms against the door casing and, with his eyes closed tight, called out, "You in there, girl?"

After a few seconds, there came a small voice. "Daddy?"

The man's face twisted. "No. Sweetie." He pushed open the door and stepped into the bedroom.

The flame from a second lamp danced atop the nightstand. The young girl was sitting up with her back against the metal headrest. With the covers pulled up under the chin of her made-up face, only her head and bare shoulders were visible.

He raised his palms to her while moving slowly toward the bed. "You listen, now. I..." His voice broke and he began shaking his head. "I shouldn't be here. And neither should you, child."

CHAPTER

13

O N Monday, both the marina and the Rusty Anchor were closed. Bryce was relieved to have an extra day before having to face the old man after passing out on him. He'd had plenty of bad thoughts during his day off: Did anyone notice him laid over in the chair? Bo? Elise? A random boater? Had anyone called the agency to report him? Had he said anything stupid during those lost moments before he checked out? And worst: How the hell had he managed to drive home? But most perplexing, considering the former: Why had he raided his daddy's liquor cabinet last night? *Just taking advantage of being home alone*, he convinced himself. He was almost relieved his parents would be returning from their Argentina trip the next night.

Tuesday morning, Bryce fought the urge to bail but changed his mind. He was late getting to the marina and went straight into the Rusty Anchor. McNabb's corner booth stood empty.

"Too late, charmer," Elise said, emerging from the kitchen.

"Rough morning," Bryce admitted.

"Looks like it," she said, frowning into his bloodshot eyes. "Go sit. I'll try to bring you back to life."

"Thank you."

"Mr. McNabb left you something in the booth."

Bryce looked over and spotted a magazine on the table.

"Okay. Since I'll be eating alone, might as well have something to read."

As he slid into the booth, his phone chimed. It was a message from Katie. "You alive?"

He replied, "Barely."

She texted back. "Sorry! But it's not like you didn't ask for it."

He set his phone down and picked up McNabb's *Mountain Digest Quarterly*. On the cover, the dominant photograph was that of a faded postcard, perhaps from the forties or fifties. On the front of the card, in decorative script, the heading read, *Greetings from the Whistle Mountain Inn and Cottages*. Below that was an illustrated image of well-dressed men, women, and children, all smiling, all Caucasian, sitting or standing in small clusters along myriad carved stone steps which led up to the two-story hotel high atop the hill. It was just as McNabb described it.

Bryce turned to the corresponding page number printed on the cover's bottom-right corner and read the entire eight-page article without lifting his eyes.

There was the obligatory historical timeline of the place and the early logging town that spawned it. Next came a brief chronicling of the change of ownership which occurred in the mid-sixties. As it were, more and more of the original descendants were spending their holidays and summers in the lively bustle of Partonsburg over the remoteness and monotony of their ancestors' withering accommodations on Whistle Mountain. Hence, it was agreed upon by the co-owners to sell the property. It was quickly acquired by an ambiguous conglomerate based out of Ohio. And finally, detailed accounts from several witnesses concerning the horrific night. One contributor, a woman who had been an underaged girl kidnapped two counties away, had been brought to the mountain resort that very day to "provide services for some very nice people." Another, now an elderly and overtly religious man, had gone there that night seeking to procure said services.

CHAPTER

14

D ON'T YOU PULL that sheet down, girl," the man calling himself Winston Wakefield told her. He stopped midway between the door and the bed. "I'm gonna turn away, and you get you some clothes on. You're safe now."

He turned away and faced the small window; the girl slung the covers off her naked body and crawled across the bed toward a chair on which lay the neatly folded clothes she'd been provided. She pulled on her panties and began working the tight shorts over her hips.

The sound of shattering glass came the instant a force sent the man staggering backwards. When he was able to steady himself, he put his right hand on his left shoulder and pulled it away, studying his bloody palm.

Startled, the girl turned toward the broken window. Beyond it, she could make out a pale, boyish face in the moonlight. She watched the boy's head tilt to one side then disappear behind a small burst of flame. The man spun 180 degrees as a second round tore through his right forearm. He fell to his knees and scurried away from the window.

The girl frantically knotted the loose ends of a sleeveless shirt below her chest and zipped both shiny white boots up to her knees. As she hurried across the bedroom toward the door, a face filled the small, broken window. She let out a scream, then froze. "Oh my God. It's you," she said with evident relief. "Oh my God."

The boy's expression was wide-eyed and serious, his hair damp with sweat, his jaw set tight. "He hurt you?"

Ignoring the question, she turned and hobbled to the cabin's front door and tried the knob. It turned, but the door wouldn't budge. She went back to the bedroom and called out from the window, "Help! Hey, can you help me?" But the boy was on his way to the next cabin.

A hand clamped tightly around her calf, and she looked down to see the injured man slumped over with his back against the wall. "I'm sorry," he said, blood seeping into both sleeves of his white button-down shirt.

"Let me go!" she yelled and jerked away. She ran out of the bedroom and into the small kitchen only to discover the back door was also secured from the outside. There was a large picture window above a cheap, foldout table, on which sat a red Coleman cooler. Unable to lift the thing by its metal handles, she lifted its lid and tilted it forward, spilling ice and cold beer cans onto the floor. Then, with a loud grunt, she heaved the empty cooler through the window, climbed onto the table, and lowered herself through the opening. The soles of her tall boots found the floor of the wooden deck attached to the rear of the cabin. She scampered down the steps and hurried clumsily up the slope to the road. There, she unzipped the boots and kicked them off her feet. As she scanned the area for her young savior, she was startled by a loud *pop*. Her eyes followed the sound to a mushroom of red sparks glittering in the sky above the hotel. As they faded out during their descent, there came a whooshing sound followed by successive explosions. In the bright white illumination from overhead, she caught a glimpse of the boy emerging between cabins, heading back up to the road.

She ran to him, her bare feet thudding against the packed-dirt surface. "C'mon, let's get out of here!" she yelled, motioning for him.

Over the crackle of dying sparks, she heard him say, "Might be there's more." He worked the bolt on the rifle, lifted the barrel, and continued down the road.

She began to sob, watching the boy shuffle down the sloped front yard of yet another cabin. He paused outside its window, his profiled figure illuminated in its golden glow. With his short legs set wide apart, he lowered the long barrel. The girl heard a loud *crack* of the report and saw the boy lurch backwards from the rifle's recoil. A scream came from inside the cabin. Quickly weighing her options, she caught up to the boy and tailed him to the next cabin.

The boy went up to the small, grimy bedroom window and stood on his tiptoes to get a glimpse inside. The girl was soon behind him. On the bed, a naked man was attacking a woman from behind, his heavy torso quivering, dimpled buttocks tightening with each violent thrust. He held a fistful of her hair, her face frozen in a silent scream.

Suddenly, the woman turned her head in their direction and stared wild-eyed as the man's efforts hastened.

The boy gasped and jerked away from the window, causing the rifle's muzzle to come forward and strike the pane. Now the man looked their way. As the boy raised the rifle, the woman in the bed threw her arms over her head and fell forward just before a bullet pierced the man's temple. The entirety of his ample weight collapsed onto her back.

The woman struggled to free herself from beneath the life-less body. She rushed to the window, covering herself with a pillow. Her startled expression transformed to one of disbelief when she saw the boy standing there holding the rifle.

She mouthed something, then turned and went to the corner of the room where a small pile of clothes sat on a little chair. She pulled on her pants and shirt, ignoring her undergarments and shoes. Seconds later, she burst out the front door of the cabin.

"Gerald!" the lady shouted from the porch, then ran and threw her arms around the boy. When she let go, she stepped back and surveyed the young girl with him, her attire, the terrified expression exacerbated by black mascara running down her cheeks. "Oh God. Oh God," the lady cried. "Oh God. I didn't know, honey. Oh God, it's true, yer just a young'un." She grabbed the girl's arms and whispered, "We're gettin' outta this damn place."

More fireworks exploded over the resort followed by the rapid *pop-pop-pop* of firecrackers.

Startled, the lady said to the boy, "We gotta go, Gerald. Gerald, honey, we have to go. *Now*!"

He worked the bolt action, loading another round into the chamber, and continued marching down the road to the next cabin, the rifle's stock clamped under his arm. The lady and the girl followed. Suddenly, the dark forms of two men appeared in the road ahead. As they drew near, one of them, the tall one, the boy recognized as Stuart, his boss, who had the nice wife and drove the big white Toyota. The woman knew him as the only means of getting her and her son off the mountain and back to their home. The girl recognized the monster with whom she'd spent the past hours inside cabin five. She had sat on the chair in the corner of the bedroom as he very deliberately conveyed what was expected of her. He'd ended their session with a story about a girl, much like herself, who had made the dimwitted decision of trying to escape. He seemed to have especially enjoyed describing the resulting consequences.

The other man had the bandaged face. The boy had watched him pull the girl from the long green-and-white vehicle behind the hotel. The girl had awakened in the middle of the night to his one wide, unmasked eye boring into hers. His hand pressed against her face. The strong, sweet odor...

"No. No." The girl moved behind the woman, who held out her arms protectively.

Another cluster of explosions echoed off the mountains and lit up the sky. The man called Stuart said, "Hey, little man, won't you put that gun away, go up there behind the hotel and watch 'em shoot off those fireworks. They might let you light a few, long as you're careful." He eyed Zoe McNabb and grinned. "Right, Mom?"

The boy lifted the rifle and sent a .22 caliber bullet into the man named Stuart's gut. When he didn't fall, the boy worked the action and fired off another round, striking a little higher near the chest. This brought the man to his knees.

The bandaged one quickly raised his hands and waved them at the boy. When his associate slumped forward, his head meeting the packed dirt with a thump, he said to the boy, "Hey, that's good shootin', son. Who taught—"

"My Grammy said y'all was evil. Said y'all's hurtin' girls here."

The man lifted his hands higher. "Wait now, son."

"We ain't hurtin' no girls 'round here," he vowed. "Your sweet Grammy was sure wrong about that. No, no...we're *workin'* girls. I betcha that's what she said." He craned his neck, looking beyond the three of them, then returned his exposed eye to the boy. "You just didn't hear straight."

The boy's mouth grew small and tight. His body pulsed with each quick, shallow breath, the rifle aimed and ready.

The bandaged man began taking tiny, nearly imperceptible steps forward. With his raised hands still affecting submission, he said, "Nah, see, we give 'em a chance to make a livin'. That's what your pretty mama was doin' here, just a little work during our busy time so she can make enough money to get you off this mountain. Get you and her back home."

"Don't you dare," Zoe McNabb spat. "I'm here of my own choosin'. This little girl didn't make no choice to be here. How many more—"

A scuffing sound came from behind them; the woman and the girl both spun around. The strange little man with a limp and the crazy shirt was coming at them, his head bobbing sideways as he wobbled down the middle of the dirt road.

The boy remained focused on the bandaged man. "Why we wanna get off this mountain? This's where we live."

"Gerald. We have to go," Zoe McNabb pleaded. "Gerald!"

"No, no, son," the man continued, his one visible eye still flitting from foreground to background. "Now that your grandma's gone, God rest her soul, that land you're livin' on belongs to the government, see?"

The man on the ground with two oozing wounds in his torso let out a low moan. His colleague glanced down at him and said matter-of-factly, "You hush up, Stu. I'm havin' a discussion with this bright young boy." He raised his head, then tilted it and gave a slight nod. "See, they gonna run y'all off. And all that land of your grandma's? I'm 'fraid it'll just be a few more acres for the bears to poop on." He let out a forced chuckle.

"My Grammy wasn't wrong 'bout you," the boy said. "I *seen* you drag that girl down here. I seen that man hurtin' my mama. Yer evil. So, mister, I'm gonna send ya to hell 'cause Grammy said that's where yer kind belong."

The man grinned and extended an index finger. "Easy now, son. Hold yer fire." He gingerly loosened the white bandages from his face. A flurry of fireworks exploded overhead as the soiled strips of gauze fell to the ground. The skin underneath shone pink in the light of the flickering embers, with areas resembling melted candle wax. The newly exposed eye was swollen shut. "Wanna see more?" he teased.

The boy glanced quickly toward his mama and the girl, who were still watching Gaspar coming toward them.

"Lookie here," the burned man chided. "Look!"

The boy turned back to the man who was now lifting the funny looking hat from his head, revealing a scalp covered in dark-red patches with sparse strands of hair sprouting wildly. He took another few steps toward the boy, leaned down, and lowered his head to give his young accuser a better look at his recently amassed injury. Then he straightened and said, "See, son? I done swam in the fiery lake of hell. But I's so mean...well, the Devil sent me back."

"Gerald!" Zoe McNabb screamed as Gaspar raised a pistol at them.

Several quick pops rang out, sounding like another string of firecrackers igniting. Gaspar's body twitched. He turned and pointed his gun in the direction of the wooded slope between the dirt road and the hotel. A single flame burst from the gimp's hand, then another quick succession of rounds from a concealed shooter. Gaspar turned back toward them and, as if controlled by an amateur puppeteer, managed a few rickety steps before buckling into a lifeless heap in the middle of the road.

Gerald turned back around to discover the burned man

had drawn ever nearer. "You're lucky, son," he said, an uncanny smile spreading across his disfigured countenance. "All these fireworks going off. *Pop, pop! Bang, bang!* Stu and I thought we'd step outside our little office down there and enjoy the spectacle."

He took a few unhurried steps toward the boy. "Why, had I known there was a gun-totin', snot-nosed nipper like you goin' around shootin' up my customers…"

Gerald worked the bolt action and pulled the trigger. *Click.*

"I'd have brought my own fire stick out here with me," the burned man continued, now taking quick strides toward the boy, "and blowed your fuckin' little head off!"

He lunged for the rifle and grasped its barrel, causing Gerald's finger to involuntarily pull the trigger. This time, the mechanisms, long sullied by age and elements, managed to establish the necessary connections to discharge a slug that created a tiny dot just beneath the man's up-turned chin. He fell to his knees with one hand still clenched around the barrel. Gerald McNabb worked the bolt action one last time, sending a second round into the man's skull just as a thunderous eruption sent points of multicolored lights raining down over the hotel.

Zoe McNabb screamed, "Oh, my God!"

A vehicle's headlights illuminated the gruesome scene. The living turned to see the white Toyota Land Cruiser bounding toward them. It skidded to a stop. A woman leapt out, came around and opened the passenger door, then the door at the rear of the vehicle with the spare tire attached.

"C'mon. Hurry," she said, waving them over.

As Zoe McNabb and the two children piled into the vehicle, its driver, the woman who'd been so kind to Gerald and his mother, took off running toward the carnage. They all watched from inside the Toyota as she passed Gaspar and the burned man with only a quick glance. When she got to her husband, Stuart, she hovered over his motionless body and screamed, "You godless bastard!"

● ● ●

She drove intently, the Land Cruiser listing at each bend of the snaking road. "We need to get off this mountain. Hold tight," she yelled back at the children, maneuvering what would be their last descent down Whistle Mountain.

Zoe McNabb glanced over at the lady several times, receiving no acknowledgment in return. At last, she said, "Your husband? Stuart?"

The lady remained silent.

"He didn't make me do nothin' that—"

"I don't care why you were up there or what you were doing. I've always stayed out of my husband's..." She fought back tears and quickly regained her composure.

Zoe McNabb placed a hand on her shoulder. "Earlier today...he forgets his notebook in our room. It's all right there. In his grade-school scrawl. The cabins. Their little wine game. I've been so *naive*." Zoe McNabb squeezed her shoulder. "The Bible says..." She scoffed and paused. Then, continuing in a quiet voice, she said, "I've been plenty innocent...the part of the dove. But shrewd...not so much. I was gonna just...*leave*. Leave him and that awful place. Just...*go*. But with the fireworks goin' off, I could see down there from the window of our room. All that was goin' on. I just watched it, like it was some awful scene from a movie. I called for help, told them where I was. Hung up when they asked my name. Jumped in the truck…"

Zoe McNabb kept her hand on the lady's shoulder. She peered back at the girl sitting opposite her son on one of the inward-facing bench seats. "You're okay now, sweetie. What's your name?"

"Betsy Jo Tolliver. BJ."

"BJ, can you tell us where you live?"

BJ did, then she closed her eyes, leaned her head against the window, and whispered, "I'm okay, Mama. I'm okay now."

The road leveled off, becoming smooth and less curvy.

When BJ opened her eyes again, she noticed the boy's odd expression. "Hey," she said, and waved a hand in his face.

Headlights appeared behind them. BJ turned and squinted out the back window. There came several long blasts of a horn as the vehicle gained on them.

The Toyota accelerated. "Lord God," Zoe McNabb said, throwing her hands on the dashboard.

As the vehicle drew dangerously close, BJ noticed the grill of the truck was the same as her daddy's Jeep pickup. The driver's head came out the side window, long brown hair blowing wildly. She heard, "BJ. Honey!"

"Stop!" BJ yelled. "That's my daddy. Please stop!"

The lady veered into a scenic pullover. BJ was out the back door of the vehicle before it came to a stop. Bobby Tolliver jumped from his truck. They met and embraced for a long moment. Then BJ backed away and touched her face, feeling the wetness. She checked the palm of her hand in the light of the Jeep's headlamps. Then she looked at her daddy's white T-shirt and saw the stain on his shoulder.

"I'm okay, honey. That little creep. Just grazed me." Bobby glanced over her head. "Who's them people?"

BJ took his hand and walked him to the rear of the Land Cruiser as the two women approached guardedly. "This is my daddy," she told them.

Both ladies nodded without offering introductions.

BJ went to the open back door and peered inside. "It's Gerald, right?" Then she turned to Bobby with a look of concern.

The boy's head was raised toward the roof, his eyes wide and unblinking. A long string of saliva hung from his chin. His outstretched arms were stiff and trembling, his tiny hands with a white-knuckled grip on the stock and barrel of his Papaw's hunting rifle.

Zoe McNabb moved in front of BJ and observed her son's disconcerting posture. She leaned in and nudged his leg. "Gerald!" The boy gave no response. She backed away stiffly, scanning all their blank faces until she collided with the Jeep's front bumper. She cried, "What's wrong with him?" as a procession of swirling lights illuminated her horror-struck expression.

● ● ●

BJ clung to her daddy's arm on the long, quiet drive home, the dreaded question looming in the silence. They shared an occasional, hesitant smile. And some tears.

At last, Bobby said, "So, I gotta bring you back up here to the sheriff's office in the morning. They wanna talk to you. And me."

BJ lifted her face to his and nodded. She looked exhausted.

"All we gotta do is tell the truth," he assured her.

When Bobby reached the turnoff for Mount Jenkins

Road, he pulled into the empty parking lot of a roadside antique shop. BJ was leaning against him, asleep. With the engine running, he rolled down his window and lit a cigarette. He inhaled deeply, the nicotine moving through him like warm water. When BJ began to stir, Bobby flicked the butt across the lot and turned to her.

She looked up to him with half-open eyes. "Are we home?"

"Did anyone...hurt you?" Bobby asked, then turned his head to face out the front windshield.

"No, Daddy."

Bobby's head fell back and he whimpered in relief.

BJ was quiet a moment. Finally, she said, "How did you know where I was?"

"Uncle Terry," Bobby said without thinking.

"I can't wait to hug him and thank him," she said.

Bobby felt his gut tighten.

"I hope that boy—Gerald?" BJ said. "I hope he's okay."

"Me too," Bobby agreed. He shifted into reverse and began backing up. "I'm sorry for him. And I'm thankful for what he done."

BJ straightened herself in the seat. "I think I'll let Tucker sleep in my bed with me. But just tonight."

BRYCE'S FOOD WAS cold when he set the magazine down. He took a few bites of hash browns, then laid his napkin over his plate and secured a five-dollar bill under his coffee mug.

At the register, he paid for breakfast, dropped the change in his pocket, then handed Elise a crisp twenty-dollar bill. "This is yours."

Elise took the bill. "Tough nut to crack, huh?" she said with a little chuckle. "Hey, I'm *sure* that man has a heart underneath that crazy patch of hair. Might take a skilled excavation team to uncover it."

"I'll take your word," Bryce said, grinning. "By the way..." He raised the magazine to her. She scanned the cover, shrugged, and shook her head.

Bryce glanced at the cover himself with a sympathetic expression. "I'm afraid your ol' buddy Nabby's imagination is beginning to blur some lines." He turned and left.

Bo Shula met him in the parking lot. "Thought he might've scared you off," he joked, escorting Bryce to the security gate.

"Think he's pissed at me," Bryce admitted without elaborating.

"Oh?" Bo said, seeming surprised. "Thought things might

be goin' well. Your truck was still in the parking lot when I left Sunday evening."

Bryce shook his head.

"I wouldn't sweat it," Bo assured. "If he's pissed at you, you're in good company." He motioned Bryce through the gate and said, "You know where she sits."

Bryce hesitated above *Betsy*'s unoccupied aft deck. Finally, he called out, "Mr. McNabb. It's Bryce. Hey, I'm sorry about the other day. I hate that I—"

"Can't handle eight or nine beers and half a pint of whiskey?" The screened cockpit door creaked open. "Pathetic."

Bryce thought he caught a slight grin tugging at one corner of the old man's thin lips.

"Come aboard," he said in a weak voice.

Bryce obeyed, taking his seat in the plastic chair. He laid the magazine on the table.

McNabb grunted and sat.

They drank beers in the midmorning quiet, the only sound a quacking chorus from a flock of geese soaring overhead.

"Foreigners," McNabb declared.

"What?"

"Canadians."

Bryce smiled. He peered over the starboard gunwale and watched turtles paddling around in the greenish-brown water between *Betsy* and the dock. A few opportunistic carp glided amongst them.

"These idiots 'round here..." McNabb grumbled. "Throwin' their goddamned food scraps in the water."

Bryce nodded.

The old man lifted his head toward the sun, which

appeared exactly as it was created: a big, bright ball of fire hovering weightlessly in the heavens. He took the last drink from his can, crushed it, and dropped it onto the deck. Then dug into his shirt pocket and removed a cigar and lighter. He licked his lips, lit the cigar, and set the lighter on the table.

Bryce's ringtone sounded in his front pocket. He ignored it.

McNabb gave him a look. "You gonna marry that split-tail keeps callin'?"

Bryce snorted and shook his head. "We're...not there...*yet.*"

"Hmm. Man needs a good woman." He tapped his finger on the magazine. "You read that?"

Bryce nodded and said flippantly, "Whistle Mountain."

"Marta and me was at the flea market a few months back. Lady had a boxful of magazines. Fifty cents each. I got her down to three dollars for the whole lot," he said proudly, then took a few puffs on the cigar. "They tried to say it was some kind of goddamned *massacre.*"

"It also said the kid had a reason for his actions," Bryce placated. "A mother puttin' her twelve-year-old boy in a position like that?" Bryce leaned down and brushed something off the toe of his tennis shoe. "*Poisoning* him?"

McNabb shot him a look.

"Hey, I'm sorry. I'm not blamin' the mother. It was...you know...obviously not intentional. I mean, she thought she had to do...*that*...to get them off the mountain. But still—"

"You can skip the recap," McNabb said. "I was there."

"Yeah. Sorry."

"One good thing..." McNabb said. "Them sons of bitches are rottin' in hell. And from what I read, the big boys from out of state went to prison."

"Because of *you*," Bryce added with masked sarcasm.

McNabb gave him another look, took a drink of his beer, and wiped his mouth with a forearm. "Listen, fella. I ain't..." He propped his cigar on the rim of the tin tray, then moaned as he stood, turned, and disappeared into the dark cockpit. He came out holding the long barrel of a rifle cavalierly in one hand. "I ain't gonna be around much longer. I'd rather they not take it when they come diggin' through *Betsy*."

He held it out for Bryce, who carefully grasped it by its forestock, then laid the antique hunting rifle across his lap.

McNabb did not return to his chair. He made his way aft and stood silently scanning the mountains in the distance, which, at that moment, were more purple than blue.

Betsy. Bryce smiled recalling the young survivor from the magazine article: Betsy Jo. "BJ," he whispered to himself. He looked down at the 1930s model Remington 341 bolt action long rifle resting on his legs. Then he lifted his head to the old man standing at the stern of his beloved *Betsy*, his home. He observed the skinny bowed legs, the stained cutoff shorts, the top of his bright-blue Rusty Anchor baseball cap barely visible above his hunched back. Bryce felt his chest tighten, his face twitch. A wave of sympathy poured over him. He called out, "Mr. McNabb?"

"Mm-hmm." McNabb remained with his back to Bryce.

Bryce took a few deep breaths. His lip quivered. "I... I'm very sorry that happened to you."

McNabb turned to Bryce and gave him a doleful smirk. "Well, there's worse sagas than mine. At least I got to live a full life. That's more than some get."

The men shared a quick glance as McNabb shuffled back across the deck. He stopped at the screen door and said, "Thanks for your time. And good luck with your education…Doc. Oh, and all that talk about holdin' your booze? Horseshit. The very reason the only woman's name I utter these days belongs to a goddamned boat." Then he excused himself by saying, "I think I need to lay down," and disappeared into the enclosure.

Bryce left his half-full beer on the table. He stood and, with the rifle held vertically against the side of his body, climbed out of the boat.

"Hey fella?" came McNabb's tired voice.

Bryce stopped. "Yes?"

"Put a goddamn ring on Toots's finger."

• • •

Bo glanced up while refueling an overcrowded Pontoon boat. He watched Bryce walk stiffly across the parking lot toward his Ford Raptor, his head down, arms straight at his sides. He put something in the bed of the truck, climbed into the cab, and drove away.

There were two other boats waiting for fuel. The harbormaster checked his watch. He decided he'd look in on his lone liveaboard once the pumps were clear.

Bo entered *Betsy*'s cabin to find Gerald Aaron "Nabby" McNabb lying motionless on his bunk, hands folded over a bushy patch of chest hair.

Bo Shula's first call was 911. His second was to McNabb's substitute "companion carer," who, after picking up Katie at her apartment, had just pulled into the circular driveway of his parents' Olivia estate.

Bryce checked the screen, flashed Katie a surprised look, then answered, "Bo?"

He listened, then began shaking his head. He grimaced

and said softly, "Yeah, he...uh...said he was tired and needed to rest."

Katie took his free hand in hers.

He was quiet as Bo spoke. "Please, yeah. Let me know. And if there's anything we can do..."

Bryce nodded slowly. "That was his grandfather's hunting rifle. I think he just wanted *some*one to have it. Before he..."

"Nah, Bo. I know you're not." He sighed, then said, "There's one hell of a story that came with it."

He went quiet again, then said, "Sure, that'd be nice, Bo. Saturday." He squeezed Katie's hand. "Yeah, she'd love to. Good, see you then." Bryce nodded, then grinned. "Yeah, corner booth."

EPILOGUE

173

The Whistle Mountain Saga Comes to an End
Infamous Resort Scheduled for Demolition
By Paula Maupin

The road to the resort site was curvy and narrow—dangerously so on the few occasions we had to allow for oncoming vehicles. There were moments when the sun would brighten the green landscape and glisten off the rippling stream we followed for a good part of our journey. But a single curve would bring a sense of foreboding, with the sky growing dark and the mountains seeming to envelop us.

We rounded a final bend, dead-ending at a large U-shaped dirt-and-gravel area bordered by a dense forest of towering pines.

"Still a parking lot," he said, stating the obvious. "These days, it's used by the hikers."

I parked my Mazda CX-5, and we gathered a few necessities for the short hike. He pointed as we walked by a large wooden sign identifying the various trailheads. We followed accordingly.

Our arrow led us to a rusted, yellow gate flanked by a sign identifying the trail as that which would lead us to the site of the former Whistle Mountain Resort Inn and Cottages. It also provided a brief description of the landmark's history and warned us that no vehicles were permitted beyond that point.

My guide, now well into his eighties, had been a successful attorney in his mid-thirties on that fateful night of the killings. He claims to have been struck twice by .22-caliber rounds, one in each arm. His participation in this exposé was contingent upon my keeping his identity concealed.

He appeared contemplative as we strode past gigantic moss-covered boulders nestled within a carpet of ferns. A decorative wire fence interwoven with greenery sprouting bright-purple blooms ran alongside us for a short stretch. We came to a clearing along the bank of a narrow but lively river. A chimney and a section of foundation, both of river rock, still stood, along with huge flat stones and concrete that might have served as porch floors. Broken glass littered the grounds of the structure's remnant.

"Guess that one didn't make it," he noted, then pointed to a row of withered but intact structures a little further down the path. "Yonder's a few still standin.'"

We came upon the crumbling ruins of the tall flight of stone steps, which I recognized via online photographs as those which led up the steep hill to where the hotel had once stood.

"The long utility vehicle dropped us off here," he told me. "Then I left the others, the family, and walked alone up to the main hotel."

We then began the steep and precarious climb.

At the time of our visit, official demolition of the former Whistle Mountain Resort was to commence the following week. But clearly, its gradual, unofficial destruction had been in progress for some time thanks to Mother Nature, curiosity seekers, day hikers, overzealous YouTubers, and the suspicious fire which left only charred vestiges of the wood-framed hotel. A short flight of concrete steps leading nowhere, and the towering vine-wrapped stone fireplace that had anchored the once grand structure, were all that remained standing.

"Come this way," my elderly yet agile guide directed.

Together we carefully navigated the ash and rubble, then he stopped at the edge of a wide expanse of dirt and gravel. This would have been the rear of the hotel.

"There was a tiny barroom, or lounge, about here," he said, waving a liver-spotted hand over the ground. For the first time, he looked at me directly. "That's where I chose the girl and paid for her."

He crossed the clearing and took a path that led down a heavily wooded slope. I followed expectantly, hoping a more detailed narrative would transpire once we arrived at the location of the so-called "Whistle Mountain Massacre," which had occurred on the eve of Independence Day 1969.

He stopped at a wide dirt road that paralleled a rushing stream. "We're on the backside now, see," he explained. "Same stretch of water, just 'round back."

"These were the hunting cabins that belonged to the original members," I added.

To which my guide replied, "Guess so. They certainly appear more primitive. Shape they're in, we might could knock 'em over with a few hard breaths. Save the taxpayers a smidgen."

We met eyes for a second time, and he made this profound statement, "It's only fitting it all returns to dust after what evil took place here."

A heavy silence ensued. Then he asked, "What was it Jesus said?" He lifted his head and squinted into the cloudless sky. "'There shall not be left here one stone upon another.' Anyway, it was surely all in God's plan."

"*God's* plan?" I blurted out thoughtlessly.

He gave me a hard look and expounded, "A girl gets abducted over in Myer County. Brought up here for the purpose of prostitution by a criminal organization. On that very night, yours truly builds up the gall to break his sacred marriage vows. Over on the other side, a destitute and grieving mother and her young son living on the cusp of poverty. The mother drugs her son to sleep so she can whore herself for money to get them off this mountain. Prepares the boy an herbal tea like her mother used to make. Only she's mistaken Jimson weed for bloodroot."

"Jimson... What's that?" I asked, incredulous.

"If the doctor was right..." He scoffed. "*That* is 'bout like givin' the boy LSD."

I asked, "How do you know this? I didn't come across this in my research or—"

"He and I ended up in the same hospital that night. The boy that'd put a hole in each of my arms was one bed away, racked with seizures from the toxins poisoning his little body. Staff had no reason to relate a young boy's poisoning with a thirtysomething man's gunshot wounds. After it was determined the boy was likely havin' a reaction to some sort of ingested toxin, the nurse was able to coax the truth from his mother. At least the part about the tea she'd mistakenly laced. I could hear the conversations. Poor boy didn't know what world he was in. I could see him there strapped to the bed, bags of ice layin' all over him."

He gave me a forlorn glance.

"Had my God-given conscience not risen within me, had I gone through with it... I shudder to think... Still, I was there at the behest of my own mortal lust. And I deserved punishment for my transgression. That boy and his gun forced me to face up to my weaknesses. Renewed my appreciation for the three wonderful children God had entrusted to me. And the saintly wife who would eventually forgive her foolish husband. Most importantly, his actions, whether carried out consciously or incited by hallucinogens, saved that poor girl from ever having the filthy hands of strange men laid upon her. And...sent a few wretched souls to hell to suffer their fate."

His eyes welled up. He sniffed, removed a handkerchief from his pocket, dabbed at his eyes and nose, then folded it over and tucked it back into his pocket. He looked me in the eye one last time and said, "Now, young lady, you tell me that ain't all things workin' for good."

I did not challenge his scriptural interpretation. If the retired magistrate had come to a ruling he could abide, who was I to object?